An Academic Question

A Case for Crabbe and Crabbe

Geoffrey Foster

March 2012

Geoffrey Foster was born in London, England in 1933, and his childhood was mostly spent in the County of Kent, in southeast England. Some of the action of this book, which has occasional echoes of his own experiences, takes place in or around that area and in the suburbs of London.

His father was in the Metropolitan Police most of his working life, and his mother, when she worked, was a shorthand typist (a stenographer). He has two sisters, five and thirteen years younger than himself.

He went to public elementary and secondary school and then to the University of Cambridge, where he studied engineering. Moving to Australia in 1959, he taught Mechanical Engineering at the University of Queensland for 14 years, before switching to educational development, running workshops and other activities for academics. Eventually he took early retirement in 1995.

As well as writing, he likes reading, listening to music, solving cryptic crosswords, walking the family beagle, Kafka, and playing tennis with his sister Ynes.

Also by Geoffrey Foster:

Kit and the Beeman ISBN 978-0-9805310-0-8

Kit the Venturer   ISBN 978-0-9805310-1-5

Vincent the Beeman   ISBN 978-0-9805310-2-2

Beatrice's Birthday ISBN 978-0-9805310-3-9

Beatrice and Vincent's Welsh Adventures

                    ISBN 978-0-9805310-4-6

Trouble at the Mill: A Case for Crabbe and Crabbe

                    ISBN 978-0-9805310-6-0

But is it Art?: A Case for Crabbe and Crabbe

                    ISBN 978-0-9805310-7-7

The Problem with Janice: A Case for Crabbe and Crabbe

                    ISBN 978-0-9805310-8-4

A Medical Emergency: A Case for Crabbe and Crabbe

                    ISBN 978-0-9805310-9-1

This volume

An Academic Question: A Case for Crabbe and Crabbe

                    ISBN 978-0-9805310-5-3

Chapter 1

When Melpomene and Alex got back to their agency, 'Crabbe and Crabbe: Private Investigators', their secretaries, Marjorie and Winnie, were delighted by Alex' account of the complimentary speech by the Chairman of the Board of Finchley Hospital. And Alex added, "We have been handsomely recompensed for the work we all put in over the past few weeks, so we'll be able to pay your wages and the bills and maybe even get some more office equipment!"

"What about the burnt-out offices?" asked Winnie, "Will Mr Seaward be able to do a proper audit?"

"He assured us that he would," said Alex, "he showed us some of the files, and although they were a bit damaged, they seemed quite legible. I'm looking forward to the trial, when the extent of the embezzlement will come out! So we can close this case and press on with the next, whatever it may be."

"As a matter of courtesy, I ought to get in touch with our ex-client, Gordon Salmon, and also Vanessa and Imogen," said Melpomene, "and let them all know what has been happening, and tell them that we won't be visiting the hospital any more."

She decided to try Vanessa first. She was very pleased to hear about the outcomes of the case, but said she hoped they could still maintain a friendly relationship, even though Mel wouldn't be helping Imogen to collect swabs any more. "That reminds me, did Angela Dayton approach you over her problem? I gave her your address and number."

"Not as far as I know, Vanessa, I'll ask the secretaries – we only just got back to the office. Tell Imogen when you see her that I'll be talking to her later."

Neither Winnie nor Marjorie had taken any telephone calls, and Winnie said that she had not been through the mail since it had arrived, but would do so now.

"No suspicious brown-paper parcels today!" she announced, "Let me see – electricity bill, gas bill, council rates demand, another advert for subscriptions to that new magazine, 'Reader's Digest', and here's a hand-written letter addressed to the agency – I'll have a look. Oh, it's from a person called Angela Dayton, wanting us to look into some problem – here you are, Alex, see what you think."

1

"Cups of tea, please, ladies, before I see what this is about!"

When he had perused the letter thoroughly, he handed it to Melpomene and proceeded to explain to everyone, "She's a friend of Vanessa and Imogen, and is applying to the new Harpenden University to do a PhD. She chose that institution because there is a renowned researcher there working in her field – Miss Dayton has just completed a Master of Science at University College on something to do with viruses, and she wants to consolidate and extend her research. The expert, Professor Mark Callaghan, has discussed her proposed programme with her several times, and is very happy to take her onto his team. But there is a problem with the Harpenden people who approve admissions – they seem to be dragging their feet and even raising objections, and this is where she thinks we can help – she suspects there's something fishy going on there!"

Mel had been rereading the letter as Alex spoke, and then said, "I've been trying to recall where I heard about Harpenden University recently – wasn't that the place with the student sit-down protests going on that we saw on the cinema newsreel the other night? Winnie – could you look through the papers here and see if you can find any stories about it? We probably have several back issues of The Times at home, too, because I've fallen behind with the cryptic crosswords the last day or two – I'll check this evening. But right now, let's telephone Miss Dayton – she's put her number on the letter, here we are – can you try getting it, Marjorie, please?"

"Oh, hello, Angela, this is Melpomene, from the Crabbe and Crabbe agency – Alex and I are interested in your problem – would you like to come and tell us more about it some time soon – or we could come to your place if that would suit you better, it's up to you!"

"Oh, please come here to my lab, Melpomene – what a nice name – the name of a muse in Attic Greek, perhaps? I'm doing some more experimental work here, while I still have the opportunity to use the equipment. How about tomorrow morning – would that be too soon?"

"That would be fine, tell us where to come – we can come by car or take the tube, whichever you say is best. By the way, my Mama's name is Cynthia, so I think she just likes Greek names! Melpomene was the muse of tragedy, which doesn't really suit me – or so I would like to believe! Maybe I should have been named after Clio, the muse of history!"

2

Angela chuckled over this and said, "Vanessa has told me that you have already visited the Microbiology building at University College – I am on the third floor, Room 314, so you won't have any trouble finding me – I've got red hair! Ten o'clock all right?"

Mel and Alex found their way to Angela's office with no difficulty. It was an ordinary office, but with a bench running across in front of the windows, with racks of test-tubes, the familiar Petri dishes and a binocular microscope.

Angela got up from the bench and came to greet them. She had, indeed, a mass of flame-coloured hair, caught up in a bun on top of her head, and was slim and about Mel's height.

"I'm just making notes on my last batch of tests – I would like to get everything tidied up before I embark on my doctoral research – if I can only get into Harpenden, that is!"

Alex asked, "Just what is the difficulty, then? If Professor Callaghan is willing to take you on, surely that should be enough to satisfy the University, shouldn't it?"

"In the normal course of events, one would think so – but I'm beginning to suspect that there are devious activities going on behind the scenes. Harpenden is a brand-new University in only its third year of operation, and hasn't the same well-established procedures and structures that, for example, University College has – but that would not be enough to explain some of the things that are happening there."

"Yes," said Melpomene, "we went to the cinema a few days ago, for some of us to drool over Douglas Fairbanks as 'The Gaucho', and there was a piece on the newsreel about student protests at Harpenden – do you know about that, Angela?"

"I didn't see the newsreel, Melpomene, but I'm aware that there is a growing feeling of discontent among prospective students claiming that certain people are bribing their way in and so disadvantaging candidates with better qualifications. It's once again a case of not *what* you know but *who* you know! That's why I decided to seek professional help from your agency to sort it out – to find if there is anything behind my suspicions!"

Chapter 2

"If you were in the middle of something," said Alex, "we can wait until you've finished, we have nothing urgent today."

"Thanks, but I was only tidying up my notes – I can do that any time. When I pack up here I want to make sure I don't leave anything behind. I've got a collection of samples, too, but I've finished concentrating them with the centrifuge so they can be carried safely."

"Oh," said Mel, "now I can work out what that other apparatus on your bench is. Let me see if I've guessed right – you turn the handle and those two thingies whirl your test tubes round and settle out whatever's in them!"

"Exactly right, Melpomene! I'm expecting that there will be an electric centrifuge in my new lab, so I won't have to crank it by hand! Oh dear – I hope that this whole project doesn't fall through just because of some bureaucratic decisions!"

"What have they said, Angela?" asked Alex, "have you been given a definite statement by the admissions office at Harpenden, or are they just dragging their feet?"

"Hard to tell, Alex – here is the latest letter they sent me. It's written in such dense formal prose that it's hard to divine the point exactly – maybe you, with your legal training, can get more out of it than I can. It starts off in an expected way – *'With reference to your communication of the 19th inst., in which you apply for admission to a Doctoral programme in the Department of Medical Sciences at the University of Harpenden, we must inform you that there are still certain formalities that you have not yet satisfied, viz.: (i) the submission of a statement from the Head or Dean of your present department or faculty that you have purged your obligations in regard to the work towards your degree of Master of Science, (ii) a letter from the Senate of University College, London, certifying that you have indeed qualified for the award of the Master of Science degree (iii) your affidavit that you have never before undertaken any doctoral work at your present or any other institution of higher learning, and (iv) an undertaking that you have no outstanding financial or contractual commitments which might hamper your concentration on the work of your project. We must also point out that your proposal has not yet been certified by the Ethical Compliance Committee of this*

4

University, which is still in the process of considering it.' How do you interpret all that, Alex? I must say it makes my knees shake – I am so terribly eager to start!"

"I'm not too bothered, Angela!" said Alex, "Yes, it is couched in very formal tones, but that is completely understandable – documents forming part of a contractual negotiation need to be tied up pretty tightly, and the officers responsible for drafting it must be aware of this. Have you any reason to suspect the sincerity of any aspect of this letter?"

"Not really, but I should explain that brochures and other advertising materials from Harpenden have been deluging this campus, and others around London, for months, since the end of last term – all holding out very attractive prospects for postgraduate work, however, those who have applied have found that there are drawbacks getting in their way. In comparison with some letters I have been shown or heard about, the one I just showed you is very positive! There is also a certain amount of chatter in the refectory, and in the pub that I and my friends frequent, in which various rumours have been raised, about certain friends, acquaintances or relatives who have found it difficult to get into Harpenden."

Mel asked, "Did you regard this as simply the loose talk and innuendo that frequently get raised about powerful institutions, or have you come across specific cases which hint at underhand or illegal practices?"

"Oh, I'm glad you have asked, Melpomene – I am very reluctant to make unfounded accusations, but let me relate a story to you that I heard only last week. Would you like a cup of tea and a biscuit while I talk? – It's rather a drawn-out story –I've got a little kettle that I put on a tripod over my Bunsen burner, and I can offer you a choice of teas – but I'm out of milk at the moment, I'm afraid!"

"That's no problem, Angela – Lapsang Souchong or Earl Grey, if you've got them, but others will do!"

When they were settled with cups of Earl Grey and Garibaldi biscuits, Angela started, "I was with a group of friends in our 'local', the Duke of Buckingham, chatting about this and that, mostly that, when a man I knew vaguely came into the bar, looking around for his sister, my close friend Veronica, who is near to finishing her Master's in our department. When he spotted her, he came and joined us, and was introduced to the rest of the group – his name is Tristan Hargreaves, not that it matters – and he said he would apologize in advance for being so bad-tempered, because he was about to make some very unpleasant accusations about Harpenden University. Of course, this made my ears prick up!"

"Someone bought him a beer and he started to tell us that he had just received a letter from the Registrar saying that his application for entry into the Architecture School had been turned down. Of course, as he said, this was by no means unusual or unexpected – that school had been functioning as an independent College of Architecture for some years before its recent incorporation into Harpenden University, it is staffed by some impressive established architects and has made a name for itself. But what was unusual, and what had got Tristan's goat, was the final paragraph of the letter, which said something like, *'We understand, Mr Hargreaves, that you are related to the industrial builder, Sir Mortimer Hargreaves. If you could persuade him to direct the consultancies for some of his future projects toward our expert staff, than this would materially affect your chances of admittance.'* "

"Tristan was obviously livid – he was waving the letter about wildly as he spoke, saying, 'Uncle Mortimer is a decent man, and I would no more approach him like this than ask him to give me money – they can forget it and I'll try elsewhere!' He was red and shaking as he said this!"

"That certainly seems very questionable behaviour!" said Melpomene, "Have you heard similar stories from elsewhere, Angela?"

"Nothing specific no. But I have not yet had a chance to reply to my own letter from the Registrar, so I'm even more apprehensive now that there will be a sting in the tail, so to speak! I'm going up to Harpenden tomorrow to speak to Professor Callaghan again, and I intend to show him the letter and get his opinion. I may be worrying unnecessarily, but you can understand how I feel!"

Alex had a suggestion, "How about if we drive you up there, Angela – I suppose you usually take the train – then we can do a bit of ferreting around the University – we shall not mention your name, of course!"

"That sounds wonderful – my appointment with Mark Callaghan is at 11 am – could you pick me up from my flat at, say, 9 o'clock? I'll give you the address. Thank you so much!"

6

Chapter 3

After picking Angela up, Alex headed the Riley for the Great North Road, and they had soon cleared the suburbs and were in a more open landscape.

"The area we are going to has a number of golf courses," said Alex, "I've played more than one of them in my youth, but I haven't brought my clubs today – this is business! I looked up Harpenden University, and it turns out it is really much closer to the village of Wheathampstead than to Harpenden itself – I suppose the founders thought that that name might be too much of a mouthful, especially for foreign students. So we must look out for a signpost on the right, before we actually reach Harpenden town. We are making good time, so what say we pull off at a café somewhere for a cup of something and a snack, so that Mel and I can discuss tactics?"

"Can I make another suggestion?" said Angela, "It will save me from getting nervous about making my appointment on time, too – I found on my previous visits that there is a fairly decent coffee-shop in the Students' Union, so could we have our snacks there instead?"

Alex and Mel had no problem with this, and they were soon able to park outside the block that contained, Angela told them, both the Students' Union and the main university offices. They bought tea and some rather elderly rock cakes – the woman who served them explaining that they were lucky to get anything at all of that nature out of term-time, "We only stay open for a few post-grads and some overseas students who can't afford to go home for Christmas – but we do put on a hot meal at lunchtime and in the evening – there's no eating places in the village, except for the Blue Boar, that is."

Indeed, there were fewer than twenty other students there, though one or two started wandering in later, as a small selection of hot dishes was brought out and put in the counter display.

At the table, Melpomene explained that she and Alex had talked the previous evening, and they had decided on a two-pronged approach, "I shall just ingratiate myself with whichever students will talk to me in the Students' Union or around the campus – I'm not so elderly-looking that it will seem unnatural for me to be chatting like that. I'll just play it naive and see if I can pick up any interesting gossip."

"Meanwhile," said Alex, "I shall simply front up to the reception desk and ask whether I can speak to whoever is involved in student admissions. Since Angela has told us that they seem to be keen to attract new students, they will probably have a full staff on duty, even though it's nearly Christmas, when most Universities tend to shut up shop for a couple of weeks. I shall pose as Alan Robertson, with a Bachelor of Laws from University College London, and am interested in enrolling in any Master's programmes in Law that are on offer. I shall pick up whatever brochures they have and also ask about general conditions for postgraduate admission."

Angela looked at her watch and said she had to go, "Shall we meet back here, at, say, one o'clock? That should give me enough time with Mark Callaghan."

"Don't worry if it runs later than that," said Mel, "we'll find ways of passing the time, like going for an explore or drinking tea! See you later – break a leg, as they say!" She walked with Angela as she left the building, waved, and headed off towards, Mel assumed, the biological science building. Then Mel decided she'd go for a little wander around, starting by circling the building they had just left, and then saw a group of four tennis courts, one occupied by an all-women's doubles game. She stopped and watched as they played a couple of games and finished, with congratulatory or commiserative hugs and kisses all round. Mel clapped, and one of the players said, "Are you waiting for a game?"

Melpomene shook her head and laughed, saying, "Unfortunately I didn't bring my stuff! I'm just here to find out whether I can enrol. Are you four all students?"

"Yes, we are, and we're off to the Union Bar for cool drinks – want to join us?"

The bar was on the first floor of the same building, and was nearly as deserted as the cafeteria. The barman, who looked as though he was a student too, perked up as they came in and said, "Oh good, business! What can I serve you, ladies? I'm afraid that we have run out of French Champagne right now, but we have a range of local beers and a selection of lemonades and ginger beers – or I could mix you some cocktails, as long as you like the non-alcoholic variety!"

"Just ginger ale for us, Neville, unless our guest here would like something different?"

"That sounds fine to me," said Mel, "my name is Melpomene, by the way, and I'm visiting from London. Are you all post-grads?"

The one who had ordered before said, "That's a nice name! I'm Penelope when I'm at home, but everyone here calls me Penny. These are Josephine, or Jo usually, Pam and lastly Anthea, who does not allow her name to be shortened! Anthea and I are doing a Master of Political Science, and Jo and Pam are doing a six-week qualifying programme to try to get onto the Master of Economics course."

"Oh, nice to meet you all – you can call me Mel if you like! I'm trying to find out whether there's any chance of getting onto a master's course here – I have a BA in Social Anthropology from LSE, and if there are any programmes in pure sociology or even psychology I'd be interested. But I've been told that it is not easy to enrol here and that you have to have exceptional qualifications before they'll even look at you! Is that right?"

The one called Jo spoke up, "Exceptional qualifications is right! But I would say exceptional inducements! A friend of mine is quite convinced that the academic who interviewed her here was hinting at something else – she told me he could hardly keep his eyes off her chest all the time he was questioning her! In the event, she was turned away, and now she's well on her way to being admitted to another rather more reputable college!"

Mel said, "How interesting! Is it here that there have been student sit-ins – I recall seeing a newsreel item at the cinema about protests, with marching and banners and everything, but I can't recall whether that was here or not."

"It was here!" said Penny, "I was one of those asked to join in! It was organised by a group of intending students, mostly those looking for undergraduate admission, but with some post-grads among them, who had been refused, even though they mostly had impeccable school records. The reasons they had been given were most unconvincing, like 'too many applicants from the Midlands' or 'looking for candidates with records of public service' or other weak things like that!"

"I would really like to talk to some of these people!" said Mel.

Chapter 4

"If you want to talk to the students who organized the sit-in, I can help," said Penny, "one of them lives in our Hall of Residence – a pretentious name for the ex-Army barracks hut that was moved here when the university was being built! To be fair, it's been turned into a quite comfortable place for about twenty of us – mainly girls and only a few men. If you've got the time I can take you there – I know that Pat Georgiadis, my room-mate, intended to spend this afternoon writing up her latest project – we have a communal typewriter that we pass around on a rota!"

"Thanks very much for the offer, Penny, but I've said I will check back with my husband and my friend at one o'clock, so I must keep an eye on the time! Is your place very far?"

"Not at all, we can walk there in less than five minutes – will your companions panic if you're a bit late?"

Melpomene laughed, "Alex is not the panicking type – I'll tell you a bit about him while we walk, Penny. It's been very nice talking to you, ladies – I hope we might get the chance to meet again – perhaps I'll bring my tennis gear next time!"

Penny led Mel across campus, past a couple of modern buildings, which she explained held the Arts and Business faculties, till they came to a splendid manor house, surrounded by formal gardens.

"That is the Chancellory – it is also the home of Lord Ellsworth of Hatfield, who has bequeathed his estate to establish this university. He takes no direct part in its running, but of course exerts a powerful influence. Now, before you, in perfect contrast, behold our Hall of Residence!"

Tucked in behind a row of poplars was a long wooden hutment with a roof of corrugated iron. Penny took Mel inside and along the central corridor to a door at the end. She knocked and called out, "Are you decent, Pat? I've brought a visitor to talk to you!"

They went into a roomy sitting room, with twin beds and comfortable chairs, where Pat, a small stocky woman with thick glasses, was sitting at her desk, typing. She got up and came over to be introduced to Mel.

"I welcome the interruption!" she said, smiling, "I'm going cross-eyed here – this is at least my third draft of my doctoral proposal, but I think I've got the approach right now – it's about the rise of the labour movement in Greece – I'm sweating on a grant which will allow me to visit that country and do my research, as well as tidying up my demotic Greek, which I picked up at my grandmother's knee!"

"Mel is more interested in the protest movement right here and now, Pat – I said you would probably be happy to talk to her about it."

"Certainly I would, Penny – just try to stop me! Can I offer you tea or coffee? – I'm about ready for a cup myself."

They sat down and started to sip their teas, conjured up by Pat in the adjoining communal kitchen.

"As I told Penny," said Melpomene, "I need to meet up with my husband and friend at about one o'clock, so we've got over half an hour. I'm now going to make some confessions to you, as you seem to be on the same side as us. My husband, Alex, and I are private detectives, not prospective students! We are working on behalf of a client who is one, however, and has called us in because she suspects that she is being given the run-around over her application to come here! Tell me, Pat, what successes have you had so far in your campaign?"

"Our main achievement has been simply to annoy some folk in the university administration – but that doesn't worry me over much, because it means that those among them who might have been tempted to stretch the rules in their favour should now be a little more careful! Before our first demonstration we made a point of checking the legalities – between us we know one or two lawyers, including my own brother who is a barrister, and they warned us not to risk ruining our campaign by, for instance, damaging property or trespassing on restricted areas."

"But aren't you simply making sure that none of you will have any chance of being admitted?"

"No, no, Melpomene, we who are demonstrating are all safely enrolled as students – we thought that none of us could be accused of offences serious enough to warrant being sent down! It was fairly clear that any suggestion of that would result in adverse publicity, like that in the British Pathé newsreel."

"What brought the newsreel people here then?" asked Mel.

"We have friends in the Press!" answered Pat, "The local rag, 'The Welwyn and St. Albans Monitor' is always looking for human interest stories, and we've got a couple of tame reporters on the staff. I think it was one of those who alerted the Pathé people. I went to see 'The Three Musketeers' twice, just so I could admire myself and my friends on the newsreel! And I like Douglas Fairbanks, anyway!"

Melpomene looked at her wristwatch and said, "I have to dash soon, but we must stay in touch. Why don't you two come and meet my husband and our client now and we can discuss ways of working together?"

Pat said, "Good idea, and it'll clear my head, too – I've got it full of the *Ergatiki Estia*, and the Greek Confederation of Labour at the moment!"

At the cafeteria, they found Angela Dayton sitting drinking a coffee. She jumped up when she saw Mel, and was introduced to the others.

"I've seen nothing of Alex yet," said Angela, "but it's only ten past one, so I suppose we shouldn't be too concerned."

"Maybe he's getting lots of interesting stuff!" said Mel, "Meanwhile, lets all get to know one another. Angela is applying for a doctorate programme – how did you get on with your Professor Callaghan, Angela?"

"Oh, he was most encouraging – I showed him that letter, and he said much the same as Alex, that the language was simply formal and legalistic, and shouldn't put me off at all. Then he actually rang up someone in the administration and got her to check the progress of my application. He got quite shirty with her – I think it was put on! – saying that he had to get his laboratory arrangements settled before the beginning of term, so needed to know whether this 'promising candidate' was in or out! When he finished with her, he told me he thought it was proceeding satisfactorily, but that I wouldn't know for sure until I had complied with all the stipulations in that letter from the admissions people. So I shall get onto all that the moment I'm back at UC."

As Alex was still not back, there was a general conversation among Angela, Pat and Penny, with Melpomene making notes and taking down addresses and telephone numbers.

Chapter 5

After a few minutes of chat, Melpomene announced, "I don't know about you ladies – but my stomach tells me it's way past my lunch-time. Shall we see what's on offer here? There are some nice smells anyway."

The others didn't take much persuading, and they were soon all sitting in front of a variety of dishes, ranging from noodle soup to fish and chips. Not much was said until Alex arrived and said, "Turn my back for a few minutes, and this is what you get up to! Mel and Angela, please introduce me to your friends, and than I think I'll join you – that fish and chips looks good!"

Said Mel, "Everyone please meet Alex, my husband and partner in crime-fighting! This is Penny, and this is Pat, one of the ringleaders of the student resistance movement – I'm sure, Alex, that she will be a very valuable associate in our investigation!"

Pat said, "I don't know whether it has struck anyone else, but I'm immersed in Greek culture in my work at the moment and I've noticed that almost all of us have Greek names – I'm really Parthenope, but I got in so much difficulty with that at school that I started to call myself Pat – Penny is Penelope, Mel uses her full name Melpomene often and Alexander is a Greek name, too!"

"So I'm the odd one out!" said Angela, "Unless I adopt 'Angeliki' and pronounce the 'g' properly!"

Everybody laughed happily, Mel saying, "This may be a sign from Olympus on high that we are destined to work together! But, changing the subject, what did you discover, Alex?"

"That was very interesting," he started, in between forkfuls of fish, "I went first of all to an office under the sign 'Admissions', which sounded the logical place to try. At the counter was a rather harassed-looking young woman, who wanted to get rid of me quickly, I think, so gave me a pile of forms and pointed to a table where, I suppose, she wanted me to fill them out. But I was not to be fobbed off – thought he stoutly – so I said, 'Thank you very much, miss, but I have travelled a long way this morning and would rather like to see someone with the authority to answer some of my questions.' She grimaced a little, without answering, and went over to speak to an older woman, maybe her supervisor, who was shuffling piles of papers. Then she came back and said, 'You would need to make an appointment to see Mr Benson – his office is the first one along the corridor to the right and you could speak to his clerk – but I can't guarantee that he'll see you at such short notice!' I thanked her nicely, took my forms and went to find Mr Benson's office."

"Not too promising!" said Melpomene, "What reception did you get there?"

"Slightly more welcoming this time! The counter clerk was bored rather than harassed, I thought, so she was only too eager to hear what I wanted to say. I told her that I was a London Law graduate and wanted to explore possibilities of doing a Master's in some more specialized area of law, such as commercial or international law. I said again that I had made a special trip to Harpenden because I had heard that it had a good reputation and I would appreciate the chance to talk to someone in authority. This seemed to make an impression on the clerk, who excused herself and went and tapped at the door of an inner office. She reappeared after a couple of minutes and told me that Mr Benson would see me, as long as it didn't take too long. She opened up a flap in the counter and showed me through to the office door."

"What were your first impressions, Alex?" said Pat, "I know this man a bit – in fact we've actually crossed swords, so to speak, I'll tell you about that later!"

"As I was shown into his office, he was on the telephone – he waved me to sit down across from him and went on talking. I only got snatches of course, but I thought he seemed to be excusing himself to a superior, saying things like 'I assure you, sir, there will certainly be no repercussions' and 'I shall try to remember that in future, if the same situation should arise. Thank you, Sir Desmond, I'm very grateful!' Then he hung up and turned to me, saying nothing but with an enquiring expression on his face – so I went into my prepared speech."

"Before you recount that, Alex," said Mel, "can somebody tell us who Sir Desmond is?"

Penny explained, "Sir Desmond Killane is the Deputy Vice-Chancellor – the general feeling is that he does all the work and the V-C, Malcolm McArthur, takes all the credit and appears at formal functions. Lord Ellsworth is the Chancellor, but my understanding is that the position is purely nominal and ceremonial, although I believe he does sign all the degree certificates, along with the V-C."

Alex went on, "I told him my name and my story about wanting to enrol in some Master of Laws programme or other, and then I thought I would drop in a mention that I had heard about difficulties that had arisen with some enrolments, saying that I hoped that I could avoid such problems, so maybe he could give me a few helpful hints! I was watching him carefully, as you have taught me, Melpomene, and I think I had touched a sore spot! He sat up straight and squared his shoulders, as I have seen barristers do in court when about to make a statement intended to convince a jury, and then he said, 'I can assure you, Mr Robertson, that we conduct our procedures strictly according to the protocols set down in the University regulations. If you comply with our rules, I assure you will get fair and equitable treatment!' He still seemed a touch vexed, so I made an attempt to calm him down, telling him that I realised that it was probably nothing more than rumour and uninformed opinion."

"Did you get anything more of value at that point, aside from these intimations about his attitudes?"

"Not really, Mel, but I did see that he was making notes in some sort of ledger, by my estimation over half-way through a rather thick book. I'm glad I didn't give him my real name! I then thought I would try some questions that would be less sensitive, so I asked him if Harpenden ran its own matriculation procedures or simply relied on the Joint Matriculation Board or the Oxford and Cambridge Schools Examinations Board. He answered rather smugly that a candidate could bring an assessment from whatever board his or her particular school had subscribed to, and that Harpenden would subsequently make its own decision. As a lawyer, I was itching to point out that such an approach would inevitably be the source of anomalies – but I held my tongue. I still think this to be the case, however!"

Pat said, "I'm impressed at the amount of information you've managed to extract from our Mr Benson, Alex. If everyone has finished eating, I propose that we go up to the bar and I can tell everyone my own experiences with this character over a few cooling beverages. What do you all say?"

Chapter 6

When they had all bought drinks and were settled in a quiet corner of the bar, Pat said "A few like-minded friends had got together and decided to make a protest, because each of us had met some trouble enrolling or knew somebody who had. I pointed out that we should make sure that we only involved people who were already safely enrolled, and that we should follow the advice of my brother and the other lawyer not to damage anything, nor even trespass on restricted areas. So we planned to keep to the open areas of the campus and simply march up and down with placards and chanting."

"Was it your idea to inform the press?" asked Alex.

"I can't remember who raised it at first, but we all thought it would be a good move to get written up in the local papers, so we rang up the Welwyn and St. Albans Monitor, and a couple of reporters and a photographer agreed to come and cover the demonstration. And one of them said he would telephone an acquaintance at British Pathé and see if they would be interested as well – it must have been a time with little else of note to cover, because they agreed like a shot! We settled on a Friday lunchtime for the event, to give the press people time to get organised. I had hoped that my speech would be included in the newsreel, but they haven't got round to incorporating sound yet, as the cameraman told me. But I gave a draft to the press reporters, and they printed a decent chunk of it! I'll give you a copy, Alex and Melpomene – I made sure I acquired several copies! I sent one to my parents, but they were rather apprehensive that I was getting into politics too much!"

"I can understand that!" said Mel, "My Mama would react in the same way – she has only recently acknowledged that the life of a detective is a suitable occupation for a respectable girl!"

"The day after our demonstration, I found an envelope in my pigeon-hole in the department – a request to call on Mr Benson. Naturally, I was a little apprehensive – I went straight to his office but his clerk told me he was at a meeting and that I should try again after lunchtime. Of course, I had fantasies about my case being brought up before the Academic Board or even the Senate, but when I went back, Benson was surprisingly affable. He had my student record in front of him, and when I saw my name there, my stomach skipped a beat – oh, you know what I mean!"

"Yes!" said Angela, "In your position, I would have thought that this meant that I should start packing my bags!"

"Surprisingly, all that Benson said was, 'You seem to be getting good reports from your supervisor, Miss Georgiadis – are you happy here? Is there anything I can do?' You could have knocked me down with the proverbial feather! I stuttered something about being 'all right, thank you very much', and he then got to the point!"

"Which was?" said the others, almost in chorus.

Pat went on, "He sat back in his chair, spread his arms, and said, 'You should tell your friends that if they are dissatisfied, they have only to come and talk to me!' But then he leaned forward, with his hands clasped before him on the desk, and added, 'But if anyone you know has a substantial complaint about University procedures, they must make a formal and detailed complaint in writing, send or bring it to me, and I will peruse it and pass it on to the appropriate department!' At that point, I thought that he was hoping this would satisfy me, but there was more to come!"

"He then got into his stride, 'And I would like you to go away and consider the following proposal. If you are willing, I can engage you as a liaison officer between the student body and the administration – it will not be a paid position, but I may be able to offer you secretarial or other support. If I am pleased with your work over the next few months, it might be possible for me to recommend that you receive financial assistance, for, shall we say, a study trip to Greece to support your thesis work. Please think about this, Miss Georgiadis!' – How about that, boys and girls!"

Alex was the first to comment, "A cynic like me would suspect that he was buying you off! Have you given him an answer yet, Pat?"

Penny, Angela and Melpomene all agreed with Alex' misgivings in various ways. Pat waited until they had finished commenting and then said, "Don't worry, my friends, I am not as green as I am cabbage-looking, as they don't say in the old country! I don't mind advising my friends and aspiring entrants to do what he suggested about making complaints, but there is no way that this little Greek girl is going to become his agent! And I told him this, but in as tactful a way as I could, saying that I was concentrating on library research work at present and did not feel I should undertake other responsibilities. He seemed to accept this, but grimaced a little."

"Well done!" said Alex, "you have not shut any doors completely. From what he was saying to me, I would judge that he is now feeling the necessity to step very carefully – this encourages me to press on with our enquiries. So, Pat, from your viewpoint as an insider, so to speak, have you any suggestions as to next moves? Should we approach any other officials?"

"I have a couple of ideas," said Melpomene, "see what you think, Pat. What if Alex and I approach people in the faculties or academic departments that we have expressed interest in joining? In my experience, there is no love lost between academic departments and central administrators, so we might get an entirely different story from the official line that Benson has to push!"

"So, we're talking about Law and Sociology or Psychology, are we?" said Pat, "I'm not that pally with anyone in those areas, but I do know the admin officer in Economics who looks after postgraduate affairs, so I'll sound him out about his opposite numbers in those departments. Would it be possible for you two, Alex and Mel, to make another visit here in a few days' time?"

"Only too pleased!" said Melpomene, "And, Penny, I'll bring my tennis gear with me and we might be able to fix up a challenge match – it's a while since I touched a racquet."

Alex was enthusiastic, "And I could bring my golf clubs – we could make a long weekend of it! There must be a pub in the village that we could stay at, isn't there? Let's exchange telephone numbers – do you have a telephone in your digs, Pat?"

"Yes, and I'll write the number for you – we're all used to taking messages and fetching people to the telephone. Evenings are best. If you go to the left as you leave the campus, you will easily spot 'The Hertfordshire Poacher', and you could ask them about rates and get their telephone number. Meanwhile I'll have a yarn with Tony Philpotts, our admin and see what I can fix up. Give me your home and office numbers, please."

Chapter 7

As Pat had suggested, they called in at the 'The Hertfordshire Poacher' and found that it was a nice little country pub – the landlord showed them a choice of double rooms and said that at that time of the year, they were not usually very busy, but, if they were thinking of Christmas week it would be as well to book well ahead. Melpomene thanked him and said, "My Mama wouldn't forgive me if we didn't spend Christmas at our family hotel! And we always welcome my husband's family there, too."

A couple of hours later, Mel and Alex dropped Angela at her flat and said they would keep in touch so they could arrange with Pat when they would visit the university next. Angela thanked them warmly, saying, "This little enquiry of mine seems to have grown! I feel rather awkward about taking up so much of your time, and I'm a bit anxious that the bill is blowing out rather fast."

"Don't be too worried about that!" said Alex, "It looks as though you are not the only one who we're helping, and if we find out – which looks likely – that there is something fishy or even illegal going on behind the scenes and fix it, we shall have no hesitation about charging Harpenden University accordingly."

"Yes," said Mel, "we find we often do quite well when we deal with complicated cases involving commercial or public organisations – when you see Vanessa Spring or Imogen Preston next time, ask them to tell you about the happenings at Finchley Hospital!"

Mel, who had been driving the last part of the way, waited outside the flats to make sure Angela got in safely, since dusk was falling and the street was a throughway for people leaving the nearby tube station. Angela turned in at the door, and Mel was about to pull out and drive off, when Alex stopped her, "Hang on a moment, she's waving – I'll hop out and see whether she's all right!"

When Alex reached her, she said, "I feel really foolish – I can't find my keys! Can you just wait a bit, I'll ring the caretaker's bell and ask him to let me in."

"That will get you in the building," said Alex, "but what about your flat? Do you have a flat-mate who can let you in?"

"I do have someone who I share with, but she's gone away to stay with her people in Norwich! Fortunately we have an arrangement with the caretaker, who lives in the ground floor back – he keeps spare keys for us all, but he always ticks us off when this sort of thing happens! He's a kind soul, however, despite his tyrannical exterior!"

"I'll come in with you once the door's been answered, if you like."

"No, no – that's not necessary, Mr Morehouse will see I'm safely in! Thanks ever so for your concern, Alex!"

"We have to look after our paying clients, Angela! We'll telephone you soon."

They decided to call in at the office before going home, and found Marjorie on the point of locking up as she left.

"Did you have a useful visit?" she asked them, "Nothing much going on here, so Winnie and I have just been fiddling about and tidying the file system a bit more. Oh, there was one telephone call from a friend of yours, Alex, Archie Staples. He mainly wanted to keep in touch, but when I said you were visiting a university – I didn't think I should reveal which one – it reminded him that he had an academic client at the moment who was disputing his dismissal on what he claimed were trumped-up charges. I looked up Mr Staples in our index, and we have his number if you want to ring him."

"Thanks, Marjorie, I actually have his home number in my little book, so I might try him this evening. So if there was no mail, we'll head off home. You've got your bike, I suppose? See you in the morning."

Mel parked the Riley in the usual place in an alley next to the flat, and as she was getting out, saw something glinting on the back seat – a bunch of keys! As soon as they got into the flat, she telephoned Angela and told her, who thanked her and assured her that she was safely at home and just about to have some chocolate and go to bed.

Caroline, the housemaid, knowing them well, brought them cups of tea. "Was it a worthwhile trip?" she asked, "We just heard on the wireless that there was a bad accident on the Great North Road near Northampton this afternoon, in which a motorist was killed and a lorry driver was injured, but we knew that was further north than where you were headed, so Mrs M and I were not particularly worried, but it's still good to see you safe!"

"Dinner at the usual time?" asked Mel, "We didn't have a very substantial lunch!"

"Yes, Mrs M is making a casserole of some sort, I think. Would you like some toast or something to keep you going?"

"Just a biscuit or a piece of cake for me, thank you, Caroline!"

Alex said that he would be all right until dinner, and that he was going to try to get Archie Staples on the telephone.

It was Archie's wife Betty who answered and they had a short catch-up conversation, before Betty said, "Archie was trying to get onto you two – he's just picked up a case that might appeal to you – I'll put him on."

"Oh, thanks for ringing, Alex – first of all, congratulate me – I'm now a silk and can put KC after my name! And practically the first case that's come my way is a guy who's being given the push from his lectureship at our old Alma Mater – University College, so I thought that might interest you, especially since your secretary mentioned that you two were involved in some university problem. It's not at UC, is it? – That would be too much of a coincidence!"

"No it's Harpenden – a somewhat different league from UC! What is your client charged with, if it's OK to ask?"

"Perfectly all right – you can read all the details in the Law Society Reports – he's already been committed for a hearing, which will come up in a week or two – unless they put it off over the Christmas season. He's been accused by several female students – by the way, particularly appropriate in the circumstances, one could say, in the Department of Romance Languages – of sexually molesting them, trying to have his wicked way with these young ladies!"

"Are you going to rely on the traditional defence in these cases, that the girls were 'asking for it' or 'dressed in a provocative way' or were known to be of 'ill repute', Archie?"

"Not at all – I shall claim that he is being persecuted by a rival!"

Chapter 8

"That is very intriguing!" said Alex, "So much for the academic tradition of civilized collaboration! Tell me more, Archie, as far as you know, did he actually do anything wrong, or is this rival setting it all up by inducing the students to make false accusations?"

"To tell you the truth, Alex, I'm still making up my mind. So far I've interviewed Colin Winston, the defendant – he's a lecturer in Spanish and Portuguese – and I've spoken to his head of Department, Professor Bland, but as a barrister I'm limited in what I can do, so I'm relying on what these two have said. To be fair, the professor is behaving quite properly and not being accusatory, but he has to take his responsibilities for the care of his students seriously."

"What you need, Archie, is to call upon the services of a reputable investigation agency – I think I could suggest a suitable one! What is needed is to assemble information from a variety of sources – the rival and other academics in the department, the plaintiffs and other students, the HoD, and of course Mr Winston – or is it Dr Winston?"

"You've got me thinking, Alex – and if there happened to be a female detective involved, she would be the best person to interview the young ladies in question!"

"Right, Archie, let's all get together in a day or two and work out a plan of campaign. Your schedule is probably more constrained than ours, except that we have promised to make a visit to Harpenden over a long weekend soon. Melpomene sends her regards to you and Betty – she's been listening on the extension. This all sounds very entertaining!"

"Can you tell me what your case at Harpenden is all about, Alex? Not about sexual harassment, I gather."

"You're right – except that, at a pinch, one could regard what has been happening as generalised harassment – it's all to do with irregularities in admission procedures. Our client, I believe, is worried unnecessarily, but we can understand her concern, given what else has been going on at Harpenden. There has been enough happening there to raise questions of improper standards being applied."

"Such as what?"

"For example, we were told that one prospective student had been pressured to ask his uncle, an industrialist, to get his consulting work done by staff in the Architecture school, the implication being that his admission depended on this! That was the most blatant case we've heard of, so far – many of the other problems have stemmed from the application of seemingly inappropriate criteria, such as the receipt of too many applications from certain geographical areas – which sounds crazy to me! This has raised so much ire in the student body that they have been demonstrating with placards and slogans on the Harpenden campus!"

"I suppose, Alex, that you and Mel are still looking into this," said Archie, "if anything comes to court, let the instructing solicitor know that you can recommend a young up-and-coming KC who has experience in the academic field! I am not permitted to tout for work myself, of course!"

Mel took the telephone and said, "We have made a very useful contact, we think, with a PhD student in the Economics faculty, whose thesis is centred on the growth of labour movements in Greece, who has taken on a role as one of the leaders of the student protest movement. This has brought her to the attention of an official connected with admissions, who, we think, is planning to apply pressure on her – first by dangling inducements in front of her and later, one might suspect, by putting barriers in her way. And Alex has spoken to this man, pretending to be an interested applicant. He will tell you how this Mr Benson also tried it on with him!"

"That's right, Mel," said Alex, as she handed the telephone back, "this person will need a lot of watching, and who's to know what allies he has in the other administrative departments! When I spoke to him I made quite a general enquiry about matriculation boards and the procedures they use at Harpenden for checking the performance of applicants, and the smooth way he answered gave me the the distinct impression that he was very practiced in shifty behaviour – and self-satisfied withal! And, to add to this, I overheard some snatches of a telephone conversation he was having with a superior, maybe the Deputy Vice-Chancellor, in which he seemed to be applying a fair layer of soft soap – this is the sort of chap who, when he shakes hands, makes you inclined to count your fingers!"

"Great work, Alex! We must have more discussions when we meet – I hope that it can be soon. Say bye-bye to Melpomene for me."

As Alex hung up the telephone, Mrs Mountain appeared, saying, "I can serve up whenever you like – it's beef with cheese and potato dumplings, follered by apple crumble and custard – you need something a bit heavy now it's getting colder, and I've uncorked a bottle of that coats de roan you like so much. I hope I done right!"

Not much was said for the next hour, until Mel and Alex pushed their chairs back and Melpomene said, as the plates were being cleared, "As usual, you have excelled yourself, Mrs M! I realise that's a contradictory statement, but you know what I mean! What would we do without you?"

"Have we missed the nine o'clock news, Mel? Oh, good, we haven't – I'll warm the set up!"

They caught the end of 'In Town Tonight; and then there were the six pips and the announcer said, "London calling, here is the news ..." The only items of any interest were a forecast of snow in the Lancashire and Cheshire areas, and a report that there had been a number of burglaries recently in North London, "The Metropolitan Police are advising householders in the area to double-check their outside doors and especially French windows, as two of the break-ins have involved the breaking of glass. What was taken, in general, were small items of jewellery and some cash. Enquiries are proceeding and a police spokesman told the BBC that they hoped to be able to announce arrests shortly. Our next programme is a concert of dance music presented by Joe Loss and his band from the Hammersmith Palais."

The strains of 'In the Mood' were heard, and Mel and Alex relaxed and listened to the music until Alex said, "If you're going to doze, Mel, you would be more comfortable in bed!"

So they had a cup of chocolate each and went to have a bath before retiring.

"I'll check the front doors and windows," said Alex, "and I'll ask Caroline and Mrs M to do the same at the back. I don't want to have to confront burglars tonight!"

Chapter 9

After breakfast, Melpomene and Alex were just about to set out for the office, when Pat telephoned from her digs, "Good morning, Alex, Pat Georgiadis here. I'm going into the department this morning, and I'll try to get to talk to Tony Philpotts, our administration officer. I thought I would ask him general questions about admission procedures, but while I'm about it, have either of you any specific questions I should put to him?"

"Good thinking, Pat – ever since I spoke to dear Mr Benson, I've been doubting his claim that Harpenden would happily accept any matriculation assessment that a candidate chose to bring in. Could you ask your Mr Philpotts, maybe in some sort of indirect way, what the real criteria are? What certificate did you submit yourself, Pat?"

"I had a perfectly usual matric – from the Oxford and Cambridge Schools Examinations Board, as far as I remember. I went to Guildford Girls' Grammar, and that was the one they put us in for – we girls had no choice, of course. Maybe I'll start by mentioning that to Tony and then asking naïve questions, to find out whether he or his colleagues in other faculties have heard of people having those sorts of problems – he's aware that I've been involved in the demonstrations."

Mel, who had been listening, took the telephone and said, "If you get a chance, Pat, perhaps you could work into your conversation the subject of improper behaviour – ranging from apparent prejudice on the grounds of social class, or even race or religion – was your Greek family background ever mentioned, for instance? And all the way to any suggestions of overt sexual advances! We have heard that such things are known to take place in institutes of higher learning, would you believe!"

"Not only higher learning, Mel, I can assure you! A few years ago there was a huge scandal at my school, that resulted in a young groundkeeper being sacked – but not charged – and a girl leaving under a cloud! The general chatter amongst us girls was that whatever happened was instigated by the girl, not the young fellow, but nobody really knew for sure! The shrubbery was replaced by flower beds after that!"

"Thanks, Pat – let us know what you find out." said Mel, "For our part, we are going to make sure that Angela's response to her letter from the admissions people has all the i's dotted and the t's crossed – Alex will apply his legal eagle skills to that – so that if there are any further criticisms they will not be due to shortcomings in her drafting. It'll be interesting to see how it's received this time round!"

While Melpomene was on the telephone, Alex had been looking through the papers – The Times, which they took mainly for Mel's cryptic crossword, and The Trumpet, which covered stories of a more mundane or sensational kind.

"That's interesting!" he said, "The Times has picked up the student protest story from that local paper, the Welwyn and St. Albans Monitor, and used it as the basis of an opinion piece about the 'doubtful standing of some of our Johnny-come-lately centres of higher education'! At a guess, the columnist who put this together is either a smug product of Oxford or Cambridge, or someone who failed to get into either!"

"What's his main theme?" asked Mel, "I assume he's a male – any female reporter who has managed to make her escape from the women's pages would not be likely to risk being controversial, I would imagine."

"Perhaps we'll see if we can find out who wrote it, Mel. But it certainly expresses some strong views! He claims that the younger universities, especially in the provinces, are suffering from an inferiority complex, which induces them to become excessively self-critical with their admission procedures on the one hand, and their graduation standards on the other. He mentions the case of 'an acquaintance' who was denied a first-class degree and had to be content with a second, simply because his department thought they had already awarded too many firsts. Would you believe it?"

"What about admissions, Alex? Does he quote any dubious examples of enrolment decisions?"

"Yes, listen to this – it could easily be Harpenden, though he's careful not to name names, *'A nineteen-year-old woman, hoping to enter a Sociology course at a college in the Home Counties, was refused on the grounds that, although her academic results were exemplary, she had not played sports nor belonged to any clubs at school, and so was psychologically unfitted for a course fundamentally based on human interactions'*. How arrogant can you get, Mel?"

Alex carefully cut out the article, to be put away with other documents in the case, and said, "Another cup of tea, my dear, and we should go to the office. Bring The Trumpet with you, Mel, and we can see whether they have anything relevant as well."

As they went down the stairs to the street, there was a knot of people round the door of the ground-floor flat. Mrs Hilton, their neighbour, was talking to a policeman who was taking notes, and when she saw Mel and Alex she said, "You should check your back door to the outside stairs – we had a break-in last night! They must have been frightened off, because we don't think they managed to get in – just smashed one pane in our side window to try to reach the handle. Fortunately it's painted stuck – I've been nagging Stan for ages to fix it, but he's kept putting it off, thankfully, so I'll forgive him this time!"

The policeman tipped his hat to Alex and Mel and said, "I've got a CID man coming to check for prints, Mr and Mrs Crabbe – I don't think this crime is serious enough for your agency! These merchants have been trying it on all around here – they had a go at the fruit shop up the street a couple of nights ago, but the beat copper spotted 'em and they did a bunk – one of these days we'll collar 'em! All the same, it wouldn't be a bad idea to check your doors and windows before long."

They thanked the PC and told a reporter, who spoke to them as he was arriving, that he should check with the police as they didn't know anything.

Mel grabbed Alex' sleeve as they reached the Riley, "We'd better have a good look round the car – one of the problems with a tourer is that the top is easily slashed."

Nothing appeared to have been disturbed, so they drove straight to the office and then told Marjorie and Winnie about the excitement.

"It's been happening here, too!" said Winnie, "When I went for the milk and jam tarts, Mrs Jenkins told me that her back window had been smashed in the night. It's only the shop store-room – whoever it was had just eaten a few things, like cheese. And the police detective told her that this showed they were only amateurs – any serious crooks know that people have been traced from the bite-marks they've left behind in cheese or even apples! I shall have to remember that next time I burgle anywhere, and make sure to finish off everything I try!"

Chapter 10

Marjorie said, "Cups of tea, as usual? Here are some letters to look through while I put the kettle on."

The only items of business interest in the mail were one from the Registry of Firearms, informing both Mel and Alex that their certificates to carry pistols and purchase ammunition would need to be renewed soon, and another that was a summons for them to appear as witnesses in a case of embezzlement and arson at Finchley Hospital, at a date early in the new year.

Apart from those, there was a very early Christmas card from Detective-Inspector Jimmy Manley 'and everyone at Mile End Road nick!' and one with French stamps – which Winnie claimed for her brother's collection – that enclosed another card, with a congratulatory message from their friend, Hugo Palance at the Sûreté and a clipping from a Paris newspaper, headed *'Trafiquant de drogues arrêté à Calais'*, which tied up another loose end for Crabbe and Crabbe.

"Any telephone messages?" asked Alex.

"Not really," said Winnie, "except that a man rang ten minutes ago asking for 'Mrs Crabbe' – but he wouldn't give his name and number or leave a message. He spoke quite posh!"

"Strange!" said Mel, "Maybe he'll ring back – did you say we were expected? Meanwhile, can you see if you can get Angela Dayton for me? – Try her home number first, if we have it."

Winnie found the number and rang, and then passed the telephone to Mel.

"You just caught me!" said Angela, "I was on my way to College – they've told me I must clear out my stuff today, as they have a new research student arriving. I shall also go to the departmental office and get the rest of the documents that are needed for my Harpenden application. Would Alex be able to run his eye over them for me? – I don't want them to be returned for changes! Would this afternoon be all right, Mel? I have some boxes of test-tubes and other stuff I want to leave in the flat, so I'll probably take a taxi home and then come on to you by tube."

"Of course, Angela – take your time and then bring all the paperwork here. We can talk about our next moves at Harpenden, too. See you then!"

As Melpomene hung up, she was beckoned by Winnie, who was holding the other telephone. She covered the mouthpiece with her hand and said, "It's that mysterious man with the posh accent!"

Mel took it and said, "Mrs Crabbe here – did you want to speak to me? But perhaps you could first tell me your name, and what you are concerned about?"

"Yes, madam, I certainly will – I think you need to be told something important before you and your husband pursue your enquiries at Harpenden University any further. My name is Cyril Speedie, and I am the personal assistant to Sir Desmond Killane, the Deputy Vice-Chancellor. I was acting as minutes secretary when Miss Dayton was interviewed by our Registrar, Mr Jupes, and Professor Callaghan on her first visit to the campus, almost two months ago. I should say that Mark Callaghan was sufficiently impressed with her that, after the interview, he convinced Mr Jupes to allow her to go ahead with her application. She was advised to that effect before she left. As far as I knew, that process had been proceeding smoothly, so I was puzzled later on to find out that she had seen the need to engage your agency, Mrs Crabbe! You may wonder how I knew about that, since you have been giving false names!"

"Yes I am certainly puzzled – how did you discover this, Mr Speedie?"

"Patience, please, Madam! I am about to explain – my previous career as a civil servant in the Ministry of Education has left me with a tendency to long-windedness, I fear! My colleague, David Benson, rang me up and said that I should be on the lookout for someone calling himself Alan Robertson and purporting to be making enquiries about enrolling in the law faculty here. He said that this person seemed far too self-confident to be a candidate for admission, and was asking the sort of questions that Benson did not think would occur to anyone in that position. I merely made a mental note at that time and took no action."

"What happened next? – I am becoming quite intrigued!"

"My discovery of your real identity came about because I was having a quiet drink at the 'Hertfordshire Poacher' public house when you two and Miss Dayton came into the public bar and spoke to the landlord, who I know quite well. I recognised her immediately, and wondered who her companions were. I make no apologies for my inquisitiveness, since you were being deceptive first! I made some remark to the landlord after you had left, saying that I was wondering about you, and he showed me the business card you had left with him."

"You sound as though you might have the makings of a good detective yourself, Mr Speedie!" said Melpomene, "I suppose you would really like to know why Miss Dayton engaged us – however, as you would well appreciate, I'm afraid that this is confidential to our client, and so I am not at liberty to satisfy your curiosity! But you said you had something important to tell us – what was that?"

"I don't know how much you know about the foundation of our university, so I'll run over the main points very quickly. You may have been shown the Chancellory, which is also the ancestral home of Lord Ellsworth – every visitor gets shown this, because it's a source of great prestige for us, giving, as it does a flavour of Oxford or Cambridge or the other old universities. It is also true that Harpenden University owes its foundation to the generosity of Lord Ellsworth, who made over the grounds upon which many of the buildings are set. Unfortunately, this is only part of the story – as I and another senior figure in the administration have ascertained recently based on some diligent research by two young doctoral students – one in History and another in Law. Have you got something upon which to write? – I want to give you some references to cases that you should follow up, if you have access to a legal library."

"We have indeed – Alex, my husband, is a law graduate from University College, London, and he retains borrowing privileges to the Law Library there. May I get my secretary to take the details down in shorthand? – Winnie, can you take the telephone and Mr Speedie will dictate."

Winnie soon filled a page of her pad, then handed the telephone back to Mel. Speedie continued, "You will find from these cases, that the University of Harpenden is built, figuratively speaking, on very sandy financial foundations! One might even say on quicksands!"

Chapter 11

"We will certainly follow this up, Mr Speedie! Have you a personal interest, or are you telling us this as a matter of public duty?"

"Both, in fact, Mrs Crabbe. I was persuaded, when I joined the staff of this university, to subscribe to some long-term bonds, which I was assured would eventually provide me with funds to make my retirement more comfortable. These cannot be disposed of unless and until I leave the service of the university, am dismissed, or retire at sixty-five years of age. I agreed that a modest proportion of my monthly salary would be invested in this nest-egg, so that it would increase over the years. I am now having misgivings, of course, and I would like to help others to avoid what I now see is a pernicious trap! The legal cases I have pointed out to to you are of various kinds, but include attempts by other senior employees to extricate themselves from this scheme – mostly to no avail! May I implore you to keep my name out of your enquiries, since you will find that there are persons of malicious character involved!"

"Thank you very much for passing these matters on to us – we will let you know what we can about the outcomes of our enquiries. Be assured, Mr Speedie, we make it a principle to maintain the confidentiality of our clients and our informants."

When Mel related all this to Alex, and gave him the shorthand notes, he was very pleased. "I'll get Winnie to type these up so they are easier to read – my shorthand is reasonable, but each individual develops his or her own style and I don't want to make mistakes. I'll see what I can find in the Fortnightly Law Review – we've often found how handy it is to have our own subscription – and then I can go to the law library to get the full details from the main Law Reports."

"While you're doing that," sad Melpomene, "I'll see if I can telephone Pat at her palatial Hall of Residence."

She dialled the number and a girl's voice that she didn't recognise answered, saying "Peggy Cunningham here – who did you want, please?"

"Could you see if Pat Georgiadis is in her room, please – my name is Melpomene Crabbe – she knows me."

31

"Right-oh, I'll nick along and see if she's in – hang on for a moment."

There was a wait for a few minutes and then Mel heard what sounded like screaming, running about and general commotion! She called into the telephone, "Hello, hello – what's going on?" not really expecting an answer, but then a different female voice came on, saying, "Please get off the line, I have to call for an ambulance and the police!" So Mel immediately hung up!

She called out to Alex, saying, "There's something bad going on at Pat's digs – they're calling for an ambulance and the police!"

Alex asked her whether she had spoken to Pat, so Mel explained what had happened, and then said, "I feel so helpless! What can we do? Do we have any other telephone numbers there that we could try?"

"Why don't we try the switchboard at Harpenden University and ask for Mr Speedie – he knows we're involved so we wouldn't have to explain too much, just see what can be done.

Melpomene asked Winnie to get the number through directory enquiries and then, when someone answered "Harpenden University", she asked, "Could I speak to Mr Cyril Speedie, please." There was a pause and the operator said, "Are you sure of that name? I know of no-one called Speedie here."

"Oh, he's the personal assistant to the Deputy Vice-Chancellor, Sir Desmond Killane."

"I'm sorry, you must be mistaken, madam – Sir Desmond's personal assistant is Miss Irene Bradshaw – shall I put you through to her?"

"No, no – thank you very much – I must have been misinformed!"

When Melpomene told all this to Alex, he said, "I wonder what his game is? Either he's given us a false name or he has nothing to do with the University – or both! Meanwhile, why don't we try the number for Pat's digs again – maybe the panic has settled down enough by now that we can find out more about what's going on."

The telephone there was answered by a woman who Mel thought sounded like Peggy Cunningham once more, so she asked, "What was all that before? This is Melpomene Crabbe again – it sounded over the telephone as though you had a major crisis there – is everybody all right?"

"I think so, more or less, Melpomene – the ambulance came and the police have just arrived. When I was on my way to Pat's room before, one of the two men living here staggered out of his shared room, with blood all over him, saying he had been stabbed! The ambulance people have attended to him, and we were told it looked worse than it is – he's been bandaged up and sat down in the kitchen with a cup of sweet tea to recover. His room-mate is sitting with him, holding his hand, so it looks as though the assailant was an outsider. We'll know more when the police have had a chance to interview him – they are in their rooms at the moment, seeing what evidence they can find, I suppose!"

"What about Pat? I can wait till later if she's upset or busy with all this!"

"Oh she seems all right – I told her you had rung and she said she wanted to talk to you, so I'll pop and get her!"

When Pat came on, she said, "Exciting times, Mel! We never used to get any of this before you two turned up – only kidding! What did you want me for, Mel?"

"The first thing was to tell you about a call from someone who said he was from Harpenden, called Cyril Speedie. He put us on to some court cases involving disputes with the University, which we are going to look up because they could be relevant. Then, when we tried to call him back, to try to find out more about what was going on in your digs just now, we discovered that he had given us a false name – the switchboard operator had never heard of him, even though he had said he was the personal assistant to the Deputy Vice-Chancellor. No idea what his game is, but we're still going to look up those court cases."

"That name means nothing to me either, Mel! But I'll tell you what little I know about this assault. Eric Brown, the one who was stabbed, and his dear friend – if you know what I mean – Richard Poole, have been living here for a couple of years with we girls in perfect harmony. They are PhD students in some branch of Chemistry, I think. Lord knows what all this was all about! We're all agog!"

Chapter 12

Melpomene could hear Pat speaking to someone near by, then she said, into the telephone, "I'll have to get back to you, Mel, the police are going to interview us in turn, so I'd better get ready – not that I know much! So I'll call you later – I assume you are in your office now – I don't know how long this will take."

Mel said there was no hurry, and that she or Alex would be available for some time. Alex had been listening to her conversations with Peggy and Pat, so he didn't need to be put in the picture. Then he said, "If you'll hold the fort here, Mel, I think I'll go and look up those cases in the Law Library. The Fortnightly Digest seems to be a bit too abridged to be helpful for what we want. I'll make sure to get back here at a reasonable hour."

"Sounds good, Alex – so that I won't have to leave the office, I'll get Winnie to fetch me something nice for lunch – she often gets her own like that, while Marjorie's Mum usually packs sandwiches for her. Have fun!"

She asked Winnie whether she had made a carbon of the case list, since of course Alex had taken the original with him. She had, so Melpomene sat down at the table with the Fortnightly Law Digest and started looking for the cases. Even though Alex had said they were abridged, she thought she might find something of use. While she was leafing through she kept herself alert for other mentions of 'University' or 'College', as well as looking for the cited cases.

And then a name leapt out at her from a page – 'Speedie'! – so she read on, '*Speedie v Harpenden University: Discrimination - Evidence - Onus of proof - Two equally qualified candidates for administrative post - Whether panel's choice affected by age and/or gender bias - Need to look for indicators apart from selection interview - Tribunal failing to record findings on relevant issues of fact - Whether decision flawed*'.

Leaving aside the legal verbiage, which she thought would need Alex' interpretation, Mel came to the tentative conclusion that Cyril Speedie must have actually been rejected for the position he was now claiming to occupy and that the citation referred to an appeal he had made disputing this. The case report was dated only three months ago, and no decision was recorded, as far as she could see. "Alex will know how to proceed further!" she told herself, and went on scanning the reports.

After an hour or so, she had found only two of the cases that Speedie had cited, so felt that it was definitely time for tea and jam tarts, so she put the kettle on and went to join Winnie and Marjorie in a relaxing chat. This was interrupted after twenty minutes by the telephone. Guessing that it was Pat Georgiadis, Melpomene took it.

"So has it all settled down now, Pat? Tell me all, is the victim all right now?"

"Oh, yes, Mel, he's hardly more than scratched as it turns out – I'll relate the incident to you. He and his room-mate were both working hard at their desks. Richard Poole was using our poor old communal typewriter, and making so much clatter that neither of them noticed noises in the bedroom at first – some of our people have two rooms, while I and others have bed-sits, which are fine. Then Eric heard something and went into the bedroom, to discover what he described as a 'young kid' rifling the drawers of the tallboy. He shouted and lunged at him, but the intruder grabbed some nail-scissors that were there and lashed out with them at Eric's face and hands. This distracted him and the thief went out through the open window, which is probably how he got in!"

"Was any attempt made to catch this kid, Pat?"

"Nobody woke up to it all for a few minutes, and by then it was too late – there are all sorts of bushes and so on outside our hutment, so it would be easy to escape. Some of us had a bit of a look round, with no results. Once Eric had calmed down, the policeman interviewed him – and the rest of us, too – but as might be expected, the impression he got was very vague – a skinny youth, maybe in his early teens, wearing a green knitted balaclava and a dark sweater. Nobody else had seen him. We shall bolt our windows now!"

"Did the police find anything in the bedroom that could be useful evidence?"

"No, they checked the windows and the tallboy for fingerprints, of course. They took the nail-scissors, as well, but the policeman doubted they would find any useful prints on them, because they hadn't got any flat areas. Eric said they could keep them, or throw them away, because he wouldn't be able to bring himself to use them again! He's a bit precious, our Eric, but we all like him a lot! Now that all the shouting and tumult has died down, what was it you were originally telephoning me about?"

"I already mentioned the list of court cases Speedie gave us, I think, and Alex has gone to the law library at UC to check them. We've got a subscription to the Fortnightly Law Digest, but the entries are a bit too terse to be useful to a layperson like me, however, I still had a look – and lo and behold! I found a case involving dear Mr Speedie! It looks very much as though he was rejected for the post he is now claiming to hold and then appealed against the decision. As far as I can tell, the case hasn't yet been resolved, so either he was lying when he telephoned us, or is acting under the delusion that he actually got the job! Stranger things have happened – when I was doing a psychology subject at the London School of Economics they related the case of a judge of the High Court who was dismissed for malfeasance but still kept turning up at court and trying to sit!"

"Is there anything you would like me to do before you come up again?" asked Pat.

"No, please get on with your work, Pat, and we'll see whether Alex can come up with a plan of campaign based on what he can find in the court cases. What I'm interested in myself is trying to track down Mr Speedie – unless he really is delusional, he must have had some reasons for contacting us. Since he says he knows the landlord of 'The Hertfordshire Poacher', that gentleman might be a good person to start with. We have said that we'll be booking a weekend stay with him soon, so he should be well-disposed to us."

"If you like," said Pat, "I could talk to him, too – a group of us often go to that pub of a Saturday night, to play darts and shove-ha'penny. I could idly ask if anyone from University management frequents the place – the one problem is that we have no idea what Mr Speedie looks like, so unless he's using that name we've got no starting-point. I believe that the higher echelons at Harpenden, including Lord and Lady Ellsworth, do most of their socializing at the Blue Boar, a posh restaurant in town, but he would hardly qualify for that circle in his rôle as a humble PA, unless he is big-noting himself again!"

Chapter 13

Soon after Mel finished her conversation with Pat, Winnie asked her what she fancied for lunch, "I thought I might get a Scotch egg and something in the salad line for myself," she said, "any requests, or would that suit you as well?"

"If they've got pork pies, one of those would be good, with salad, too – otherwise be inventive, Winnie!"

In the event she brought her a pork pie, tomatoes and watercress, and all three were soon engaged in eating and chat, until Alex arrived, and Winnie asked him, "Did you have any lunch, Alex? We've nearly finished, but I could pop out for something for you too."

"Thanks, Winnie, but I just grabbed a sausage roll and an Eccles cake at the refec. at University College, so I'm OK – I wouldn't mind a cuppa, though!"

"Did you do any good at the library, Alex?" asked Melpomene, "I tried the Digest here, but as you said, the entries are very abridged – however I actually came across a possibly interesting case. But first tell me what you found."

"I worked backward from the most recent entries, Mel – looking up the cases that Speedie cited, but also scanning quickly for anything else that might be relevant, confining myself at first to the King's Bench division, where contract disputes are normally heard. Most of the cases he had listed were to do with breach of employment contract by a college or university, or with people making claims of unfair dismissal. Not all of them involved Harpenden directly, I should point out. I only went back to 1919, because most institutions would have been severely affected by wartime conditions. And, at a guess, I also came across the same case that you found, since it involved Speedie himself – a claim that he had been unfairly treated in a failed application for employment – was that the one, Mel?"

"You're right, Alex! Was there any resolution of the case listed in your fuller entry? I was wondering whether dear Cyril was denying, in his own mind, that he had been rejected for the post he told us that he holds, hoping against hope that he would be reinstated!"

"Well he should stop hoping, Mel – his claim was rejected out of hand by the court, the University's barrister even deriding it as without merit and vexatious – the incumbent personal assistant, Miss Irene Bradshaw, can feel safe in her post! As for the other cases, I noted that there were only two barristers listed as acting for the institution in any of them – Mr Francis Wilton for one action at Harwich College of Art, and Daniel Flint, KC, for all the others, including several at Harpenden, including Speedie's. I'll ring up Archie Staples and see if he knows either of these gentlemen. Winnie – have we got the number for Archie Staples' chambers? Oh good, see if Archie is there, will you, please?"

Winnie asked the clerk of chambers for Archie's line, was soon put through and handed the telephone to Alex.

"How are you Archie? How is your case with Dr Winston at University College proceeding – anything we can do for you there? Meanwhile I'd like to ask you if you've had anything to do recently with a couple of barristers, Francis Wilton and Daniel Flint, KC, who have been involved in some cases which have been drawn to our attention, which might relate to our work at Harpenden University. We heard of these in a rather bizarre way – someone rang us out of the blue and insisted on listing some cases he thought might be helpful to us, but we subsequently found that he had given us false information about his situation. He claimed he was the personal assistant to the Deputy Vice-Chancellor at Harpenden, but that is just not true – nobody there knows him, and there is another person doing that job!"

"His name wouldn't be Cyril Speedie, by any chance?" said Archie, and when Alex, in some surprise, verified this, went on, "In one of my last cases before I took silk, I was asked to act for him for alleged discrimination in appointment – I had forgotten it was at Harpenden – this guy is completely off with the fairies! He had been a fairly low-grade clerk in a regional office of the Ministry of Education and his experience there was limited to disputes between schools and tradesmen, like plumbers or electricians! I only talked to him for half an hour and declined his case!"

"It sounds as though he might be suffering from obsessive-compulsive disorder," said Melpomene, who had been listening on the extension, "he could be fixated on the idea that he is a superb executive himself and has the duty to help other poor souls who are being undervalued by their employers! You don't happen to remember his address, do you, Archie?"

"No I don't, but his solicitor would have all his details – if you like I can find them out for you – do you want to investigate Speedie, then?"

"My main aim, and I think Alex agrees, is to make sure he doesn't interfere with any of our activities. Heaven help us if he gets the idea that he is a master detective, too!"

Just then the doorbell rang, and Marjorie went through to the outer office and answered it. The others could hear she was talking to someone, but couldn't make out the words. Then she came back into the back room, staggering a little and looking dazed!

"Did you realise that one of you two – or both of you, even – has psychic powers?" she said, "One way or another you have conjured up Mr Cyril Speedie, asking to see Mr or Mrs Crabbe – shall I show him in?"

Melpomene said, on the telephone, "Don't bother with Speedie's address right now, Archie – he's just turned up! Get back to you later!"

Marjorie showed in a little, rather portly man with thinning dark hair combed over a bald patch, and a wispy moustache. She showed him to a seat at the table, and she and Winnie left.

"What a surprise, Mr Speedie!" said Mel, "I'm Melpomene Crabbe, and this is my husband, Alex – I think you have seen us before! What can we do for you? I guess that your business concerns Harpenden University in some way, is that so?"

"Thank you for receiving me at such little notice!" said Speedie, "Have you had time to follow up my information on the court cases? I fear that if the authorities get wind of what I have been doing they will try to silence me – hence my precipitate actions! For the same reasons, I have not dared to take up my position in the Pro-Vice-Chancellor's office since I was appointed. I believe that they have replaced me with a woman who formerly was a typist!"

"Forgive us if we need a little time to take in your account," said Alex, "Perhaps, if you don't mind, you can start at the beginning and explain everything to us in order. Would you like a cup of tea or coffee and a biscuit or something?"

Chapter 14

Their visitor accepted a cup of tea and a Nice biscuit, took out a bundle of papers from the inside pocket of his suit and said, "Before I describe the sequence of events that have led me here, I will warn you about a particular barrister who, I have concluded, not only appears to be working on behalf of Harpenden University and certain other establishments in his legitimate occupation as an advocate, but is also taking illicit payments to pervert the judicial system of this country."

"Would that be Daniel Flint, KC?" asked Alex.

"Ah, I see you have already scanned the cases I referred to you, Mr Crabbe! I suspect that this lawyer is a dangerous man in the pay of a criminal organization! Now I shall present you with the evidence upon which I am basing this view. I shall take you back three years to start my account."

"Before you start, Mr Speedie," said Melpomene, "would you have any objection to one of our secretaries, Miss Wentworth, taking shorthand notes? These would be for our internal use only."

"Not at all! I have nothing to hide from you – but I would not like them to be made public, for reasons that I shall explain."

Marjorie was called in and took a seat with her pad and pencil, and Speedie continued.

"As I said, three years ago I was told by an acquaintance – an old school friend, to be precise – that he had just had a disappointing experience when applying for a post as a departmental purchasing officer at Harpenden for which he had been short-listed. When he attended for interview at the time stipulated, he found two other candidates waiting – a third was already being interviewed. After a few minutes, a rather attractive young woman was ushered out by an official, with handshakes and congratulatory remarks, and then my friend and the other two were informed that the post had been filled and they were no longer required. They, of course, protested that they had been given no chance and, as they left, my friend and another agreed to seek redress. They went straight to an enquiries office in the administration building, where a counter clerk said that all they could do was to take legal advice – as she knew of no procedures in place to address such situations. I'm sorry to be so long-winded, but it is important that you are apprised of all the circumstances."

"So did they go to a lawyer?" asked Alex.

"Certainly, and the solicitor they spoke to said he would take the case on, but that he recommended that only one of them should be involved, as otherwise the arguments would become unwieldy. He said that if that approach were successful, the other would be best advised to shrug it off, rather than appeal in his turn, while if it failed this would leave the second free to decide whether or not to proceed."

"So did the case proceed to an outcome, Mr Speedie?"

"It certainly proceeded – but the outcome was unsatisfactory to my friend, and, in the event, the other unsuccessful applicant declined to go further. The university had engaged that person who I have mentioned, Daniel Flint, KC, and he made short work of the arguments put up, of the reputation of my friend's solicitor and of my friend himself, in most insulting and aggressive ways! As my friend put it to me, he felt lucky to have escaped the hearing without being charged with deliberate deceitfulness!"

"And were the other cases you cited to us of a similar nature?" asked Alex.

"Somewhat so," said Speedie, "but, of course, different in detail. The common factor was that Flint was engaged to take the institution's side and that he used bullying tactics to win each time. In my opinion his conduct falls well outside propriety, verging on the criminal. But I cannot prove anything, and if I were to try myself, I feel I would lay myself open to danger – even of the physical kind! I have formed the opinion that this barrister is in the pay of an illicit organization offering its services to whatever institution will pay it sufficiently without examining its methods!"

"Mr Speedie," said Alex, "am I to assume that you wish this agency to investigate the behaviour both of Harpenden University and of Daniel Flint? If so, I'm bound to tell you that we would need to be convinced of the matters which, as you put it yourself, are based on suspicions alone. What we need is some element of concrete evidence in order to make a start. This barrister is apparently cunning and devious, so we will need an edge in order to begin."

Mel added, "Alex is right – but I should point out that we as a detective agency often seek such evidence on behalf of our clients – in fact this is exactly what investigation entails, for the most part! Are you ready for another cup of tea, Mr Speedie – I know that I am!"

While Winnie was doing the honours, the front door bell rang again, and Marjorie went to see who it was. There on the step were two large men in white coats, who said, "Excuse us miss, but we believe you have a Mr Speedie with you. We are sorry to tell you that this gentleman has escaped from the care of the Notting Hill Sanatorium for the Mentally Disturbed, and we need to take him back before he comes to any harm."

"Please step in and sit down for a moment," said Marjorie, "and I will go and explain to my superiors, who are present talking to Mr Speedie."

She went back into the inner office and relayed the message quietly to Alex, while Speedie was busy with his cup and another biscuit.

Alex said, "I'll come out and talk to them – did they show you any authority or identification? Mel – we've been meaning to telephone Jimmy, haven't we – now might be a good time to do this, I think. Excuse me, Mr Speedie, for this interruption. I shall be back as soon as I can."

Alex went into the outer office and introduced himself, "Good morning, gentlemen – I am Alexander Crabbe, a proprietor of this agency. Can I know your names, please?"

The taller of the two stood up and said, "I'm Senior Nurse Hardwick, and this is Nurse Wellings, we're both staff members at Notting Hill Sanatorium. We should really get on with this promptly – any delay may bring about a relapse in our patient!"

"I quite understand, but we need to be meticulous in such matters. Can you show me your authority, or at least some proof of your identity, please?"

Hardwick was annoyed at this and said, "If you are going to be awkward, we have ways of persuading you!" He moved toward Alex, and his companion stood up to support him.

Chapter 15

"Just a moment, gentlemen!" said Alex, also stepping forward, "I have no intention of being 'awkward', as you put it, I merely wish to be sure that you are who you say you are. Perhaps I should telephone Notting Hill Sanatorium and verify your *bona fides*, unless you can show me some sort of identification. Mr Speedie appears to be quite calm at the moment, so there seems to be no urgency here."

Hardwick was obviously unused to being challenged, and glanced at his companion for support. Just then, the door behind Alex opened and Mel stepped through, shutting it behind her.

"Is there some sort of problem here?" she asked, "Can I help in any way? By the way, Alex, Jimmy said he will call in very soon, with a couple of his friends. Meanwhile, please excuse me, gentlemen, I need to get something from the desk drawer."

She sat down on one of the typing chairs, opened a drawer and appeared to be rummaging about in it. The two white-coated visitors turned their attention away from her and back to Alex, and Hardwick said slyly, "You're right, of course, Mr Crabbe, but we came out in such a hurry that we didn't bring our hospital cards with us, did we, Les?"

Les looked blank for a moment, but soon caught on and nodded. Melpomene by now was standing up, poised on her toes, with her hand in her jacket pocket.

Hardwick stepped forward and grasped Alex' sleeve, saying, "We can't fiddle about here no more – get Speedie out here or we'll go in and fetch him ourselves!"

Alex shrugged and said, "All right, all right, I'll go and fetch him. Keep the gentlemen entertained, Mel, I won't be long!"

He went into the back office and voices could be heard. Then he reappeared, Luger in hand, saying, "Mr Speedie declines to accompany you – sit on the floor before we plug you both!"

He covered Hardwick, as Mel drew her Beretta and levelled it at Wellings, while both thugs hurriedly complied with Alex' instructions, sitting, backs against the wall, with expressions of mingled shock and fury on their faces.

Five minutes later, Detective-Inspector Jimmy Manley, accompanied by two uniformed policemen, rang the bell and was admitted by Marjorie. When he stopped laughing, the two 'nurses' were handcuffed and led away.

"So what shall we charge them with?" asked Jimmy, "Making an unwarranted demand with menaces will do, I suppose. When we've found out more about these two we'll be able to tidy things up a bit!"

"Just to make sure," said Alex, "I just tried to telephone the so-called 'Notting Hill Sanatorium for the Mentally Disturbed', but the exchange told me that they had no record of any such establishment, nor any having a similar name. The closest they offered was 'The Notting Hill Country Dancing Society', or 'The Notting Hill and Ladbroke Grove Veterinary Hospital', and I didn't think I would try either of those!"

"Right!" he went on "Let's see whether Mr Speedie can throw any light on all this! Come in, Jimmy and we'll introduce you!"

"Mr Cyril Speedie, please meet Detective-Inspector James Manley, of the Metropolitan Police – we at Crabbe and Crabbe have worked with him many times, and you can trust him to keep confidential anything you tell him – unless it is illegal, of course!"

"Good afternoon, Mr Speedie," said Jimmy, shaking his hand, "to begin with, something you might be able to explain to me is how these two heavies managed to find you here – did they follow you?"

"I fear it was my own fault, Inspector – I left word with my widowed sister-in-law, with whom I often stay while in London – she lives in Hampstead. I didn't warn her not to pass this information on, because I had no reason to suspect that anyone would ask. I suppose that some member of the organization behind Daniel Flint or Harpenden University – or both – must have made it their business to track me down there."

"And what in heaven's name caused them to accuse you of absconding from a mental hospital?" asked Jimmy, "This seems bizarre at the least!"

"Not to me, it doesn't – you should know that the despicable Daniel Flint KC made a submission to the court to which I took my plea against unfair selection to the effect that I am, in fact, delusional and in need of treatment in a secure ward! I don't know how close I came to being committed on that occasion – I suppose further evidence would be needed for anyone to do that!"

Melpomene said, "I would like to apologize to you for some thoughts I have been entertaining earlier, Mr Speedie – I must admit that I believed you were constructing a grand conspiracy out of very little material. But now I feel much more inclined to trust your judgment! If Alex feels the same, we shall throw our resources wholeheartedly behind your cause!"

Alex nodded and agreed, "And, I should let you know, Cyril, – if I may call you that – that I have a long-standing friend, also a KC, who has said he will look into the activities of Flint and his legal cohorts for us – starting with the cases you have already brought to our attention."

"And, furthermore," said Jimmy, "I intend to dig into the background and recent history of our two white-coated friends, using the extensive resources of New Scotland Yard, as soon as we have brought a number of charges against them. We have specialist interrogators who are extremely capable of teasing out the relationships between minor villains of that sort and the webs of intrigue that often lie behind them."

Said Mel, "We need to sit down some more and find what else Mr Speedie can tell us – but first I'm in desperate need of another cup of tea – how about the rest of you? Maybe we can persuade Winnie to go and secure for us some snacks to restore our strengths, too! Any particular requests? Winnie is aware of my predilection for jam tarts!"

"Or we could go to Giuseppe's for a proper lunch," suggested Alex, "Let's have a show of hands!"

So, in very short order, after a unanimous decision, the whole party, Winnie and Marjorie included, were contemplating a rich selection of dishes at the trattoria. They chose an alcove at the back of the main room, a place, as Mel and Alex had found previously, where conversation was not easily overheard.

Cyril Speedie, by this stage, had relaxed markedly, and proved to be an entertaining raconteur of anecdotes from his previous situations, not only as a civil servant but also as a teacher in secondary schools. As Melpomene remarked, any school quickly reveals itself as a microcosm, and the members of staff are almost as bizarre as their students imagine them to be.

Chapter 16

As they left the restaurant, Melpomene asked Cyril Speedie how he got to the agency from Hampstead. When he told her he had used the tube, she offered to run him back by car, but he declined, saying, "You have all been so kind and understanding already – I'll be fine going back to my sister-in-law's place the same way. I see there's a station just up the street here. She'll run me to the railway station when I'm ready to go back home – I have a house in Hertford – but thanks very much for the offer. I've given up the idea of a job at Harpenden University – I shall probably finish up back in the Min of Ed!"

Jimmy Manley, on the other hand, accepted their offer to take him to Mile End Road police station, "My blokes took my police car, of course, to run Flanagan and Allen to the nick. I shall be interested to see what comes out of their interrogation – they may not know much about the mob who employed them, of course, since they were probably just casuals."

Mel said, "We'll drop Marjorie and Winnie back at the office on the way. Lucky we've got a big enough car now, even though it will be a bit of a squeeze!"

When they drew up in their normal spot in the station yard, they saw a policeman waiting, who came over and spoke to Jimmy, saying, "Thought you'd like to know straight away, Inspector, that the fingerprint boys are swarming over the stolen ambulance that the two so-called nurses were using. They had left it on the street opposite Crabbe and Crabbe, and it had already appeared on our stolen vehicles list. Most of the prints would match the two we've already collared, and of course the regular crew from the hospital, but there's an off-chance they'll find something interesting."

Jimmy told Mel and Alex that of course he would keep them informed, and "Thanks for the late lunch and entertainment!"

As they walked back into the office, Alex snapped his fingers, "After all that, we forgot to ask Speedie for his address!" Then Winnie said, "Speak for yourself, Mr Crabbe – don't forget you have a highly-efficient secretarial staff here – while you two were tackling the villains, I occupied Mr Speedie by getting his details – his address in

Hertford, his sister-in-law's address in Hampstead, and telephone numbers for both. They are all safely entered in the index book!"

"How could I doubt you, Miss Morris? What a joy it is to have employees like Marjorie and you! Now, what were we doing before Cyril interrupted us?"

Winnie knew this, too, "You were talking on the telephone to your friend Archie Staples – and you cut him off when Mr Speedie arrived."

"Yes, that's right! I'd better speak to him – there's a lot to explain! Can you see if he's still available, Winnie, please?"

The chambers clerk told Winnie that Staples KC was in court just now, but was expected back within the hour. "I'll mention your call to him, would you like him to return it? It's Crabbe and Crabbe, is it not?"

So, when the telephone rang later, just as everyone was thinking of packing up and going home, they all thought it would be Archie, so Alex picked it up. But instead, he heard the familiar voice of Jimmy Manley.

"Sit down, Alex, I have a severe shock for you. Cyril Speedie's body has just been recovered from the lines at Finchley Road tube station. He must have been waiting for a connecting train – a woman saw him standing there and then, she says, someone deliberately pushed him off the platform as a train approached. She is in shock and is being looked after in the station office, with a policewoman standing by to interview her when she has recovered sufficiently. The stationmaster had his wits about him, and asked anyone else who might have seen the incident to wait until the police came. The guys from the North Finchley nick arrived very promptly, I'm glad to say, and their station-sergeant called me. There are two men and a woman who said they were prepared to talk about it, as well as a young lad. Do you or Mel want to take part in the interviewing? If so, you will have to be quick, we can't reasonably detain these witnesses for very long. Fortunately it's going-home time, so none of them are too worried about the delay. They've been allowed to use the station telephones to ring home if they wished. One woman has taken advantage of this."

"Has anyone informed his sister-in-law?"

"No, Alex, because we don't have her telephone number. If you have, please give it to me and I will see to it. He was identified from his driving-licence."

"Very well, Jimmy, we'll get there as soon as we can. Finchley Road underground station, you say. Should we ask for the station-master's office, or what? Here is that number you wanted."

In less than twenty minutes, Melpomene and Alex were at the station. Outside was an ambulance waiting, with a covered stretcher being loaded aboard. Mel, showing her police warrant card, asked the attendant where it was being taken, "North Finchley Hospital for the necessary post-mortem," was the answer, "but the cause of death is fairly clear, he was pretty much cut to pieces!"

Inside, Jimmy was being shown to the office, so they followed him and were all introduced to the station-master by the uniformed sergeant who had taken charge, who, interestingly, already knew both their names! In a small adjacent room, a policewoman was patting the hand of a woman, who was still pale and trembling, but gestured to Jimmy, saying, "If you're the one in charge, I'd better tell you now, before I forget anything!"

She described what she had seen in great detail, even to a description of the assailant, "He wasn't a big man, but stocky, and he seemed to be waiting for just the right moment. He was staring fixedly at the poor man and lunged forward and pushed him just as the train came toward the platform. It was still moving when he fell in front of it. I don't suppose a train like that can pull up very quickly! I was an ambulance driver in the war, so I know about these things! I didn't see them pull the victim onto the platform, but as soon as he was up I could see that he was finished – as I said, I was an ambulance driver! The assailant was wearing an ordinary blue serge business suit, polished black shoes, no hat, but a maroon woollen scarf round his neck and the lower part of his face. Thick horn-rimmed glasses, and brown leather gloves. You see a hundred like that on the street every day, I'm afraid! I work as an advertising artist, so I look at people!"

"That was exceedingly useful, Madam," said Jimmy, "please leave your address with the sergeant here. Thank you so much!"

Chapter 17

They all went back to the station office, where the other witnesses were filling out standard incident report forms. Melpomene said, "Can I talk to this young fellow first?" and led the lad, about eleven or twelve years old, to another seat at the side of the room.

"Can I see your report first, please? That looks very neat, Charles, or do you prefer Charlie? I'm Mel Crabbe, a private detective, like Sexton Blake, and I'd like to ask you some extra questions. We have already been told what the man who did the pushing looked like, and how he was dressed, but what I want to ask you is did you notice him before he pushed the poor man?"

"Yes, Miss, I was looking at him because he was fidgeting about uneasily and peering around a lot, and then he spotted the gentleman who he was going to push and worked his way nearer him – there was a lot of people on the platform, so he was saying, 'excuse me, excuse me' and pushing past them. Nobody seemed to mind, because it's always like this at rush hour."

"Did he have anyone else with him, or couldn't you tell?"

"Yes he did, actually! There was a tall gent in a long grey raincoat standing against the back wall, and the pusher glanced at him as soon as he spotted his victim, and got the nod! They must of been members of the same gang!"

"He was tall and in a grey raincoat – what else can you tell me about him?"

"He was nearly bald but had a little mo – his nose was very big and red, and he kept pulling at his ear! He was carrying a rolled-up brolly, black."

"Did you see this pair again after the man was pushed off the platform?"

"No, miss, I was too busy watching the underground men climbing down and getting hold of the dead man. You could see he was dead, straight away."

"That was very helpful, Charlie. If you think of anything else, please write it on your witness form there."

Between them, Mel Alex and Jimmy interviewed the other witnesses, but only one of them, a woman, had noticed the second villain, and recollected that he and the pusher were nowhere to be seen after the victim was retrieved.

"Perhaps they escaped up the stairs – I don't think they got on the train, because it had been cleared of passengers by then, and anyway it wasn't going to be going anywhere until it was checked out. The driver was sitting on a bench crying, and being looked after by a female employee. It must be terrible to run over anybody, even if it's not your fault."

After the witnesses had been thanked and let go, Jimmy, Mel, Alex, the uniformed sergeant, Phil Dickinson, and the station-master, Mr Philps, put their heads together and said that if any more information came their way, they would pass it to Jimmy as coordinator. "Sometimes people are too shocked to speak up straight away, but volunteer extra stuff later," said Jimmy, "it's possible they might telephone either the police or the Tube authorities. Maybe there'll be nothing, but we should stay receptive. Thank you, Mr Philps – we appreciate it when people outside the force are so cooperative!"

Melpomene and Alex decided to go straight home, thinking that as they were packing up when they took the fateful call, Marjorie and Winnie would have gone home too.

This was a good guess – as they let themselves into the flat, Caroline said that Marjorie had telephoned and given them the bare facts, so over the inevitable cups of tea, Mel and Alex brought her and Mrs Mountain up to date.

"There was a piece on the six o'clock news, too – simply saying that a passenger had fallen under a tube train at Finchley Road – no name or other details!" said Caroline.

"I'd better telephone Mama, then, otherwise she might jump to conclusions, since that's not far from here or the office, and she tends to assume the worst!" said Mel and proceeded to speak to Lady Cynthia and put her mind at rest.

"We'll see if the BBC has any more at nine o'clock," said Alex, "we must remember to switch it on!"

Mrs M called them for dinner then, and they eagerly tucked into a meal of pea-and-ham soup followed by lamb cutlets, their lunch being by then but a faint memory.

The only extra information on the later news was the name and personal circumstances of the deceased, said to be an unmarried civil servant, thirty-six years old, of Hertford.

"I assume that they informed Cyril's sister-in-law, otherwise they wouldn't have released his name," said Alex, "I'd better get onto Archie Staples and tell him the full story – he must be in somewhat of a state of suspense since I spoke to him this afternoon!"

When Archie had heard the story, he said, "I may have a suspicious mind, but my immediate thoughts were that since the poor fellow turned out not to be paranoid after all, the notorious Daniel Flint KC might well be involved. The idea of sending some so-called psychiatric nurses after Mr Speedie could only have come from someone who had already questioned his sanity – and that seems to have been one of Flint's favourite courtroom strategies. And when that effort was foiled by the actions of a well-armed pair of perspicacious investigators, the second string was brought in. You know, Alex, this has made me even more resolved to find out more about my not-so-esteemed fellow Silk! And it very much looks as though he's working with a criminal organization – you two had better watch your backs and avoid standing near the edges of platforms!"

"Thanks, Archie!" said Alex, "I'll pass your thoughts on to Jimmy Manley – between all of us we'll need to come up with a plan of campaign – we can't leave it to the forces of evil to make the next move. Melpomene and I will make sure we keep our pistols handy at all times! We were very lucky to be able to put our hands on them so easily this afternoon!"

"Very good, Alex – keep in touch. Meanwhile I'll see what more I can discover about the rogue barrister – did I tell you he's actually a member of my chambers? I will have to be very circumspect – if I've got access to his background and activities, the converse is true for him!"

Alex rang off and relayed the main points to Mel.

"Who else should we recruit?" she said, "It doesn't seem to fall into the areas that Hugo Palance, Jens-Olle Pedersen or Adrian Fitz-Hugh are interested in, but it might not be a bad idea to ask them for ideas, all the same. Any others spring to mind, Alex? Has Flint appeared in the Northampton or Huddersfield areas, for instance? We have good friends in high places there."

51

Chapter 18

The next day at the office felt like somewhat of an anticlimax, and Mel and Alex found it hard to concentrate, so Alex suggested they might as well go and visit Pat Georgiadis and the others at Harpenden University right away, instead of waiting for their planned long weekend.

"Let's see if Angela wants to go too," said Melpomene, "you could check all her admission documents as you said you would, and if they are all complete and correct she can hand them in personally. I'll give her a call and see what she thinks of that idea. And I'll check with Pat too, to make sure she is available this afternoon."

As it happened, Pat said she was glad they had called, because she had something quite interesting to tell them, "Don't get your hopes up too high, though! It may or may not help a lot in your enquiries. You'll be able to tell when you get here. Are you setting off soon? Right, I was going to go into town for some supplies, but I'll leave it until after lunch now."

After these calls, they picked up Angela and were soon heading for Harpenden University. On the way they related the story of Cyril Speedie to her – she had neither heard the BBC News, nor read the story that had appeared in most newspapers that morning, so she was simultaneously fascinated and horrified.

"This causes me to wonder who else might be in danger, Mel and Alex – what do you reckon was the motive of the pusher and his companion? What could they have had against poor Mr Speedie? He might have been behaving a bit crazily, but he sounded inoffensive enough!"

"I've been thinking," said Melpomene, "perhaps the opposition – whoever they are – got wind that he was taking his concerns to us in the first instance and were apprehensive that he might approach the police next. We concluded that he was putting together a dossier about Daniel Flint KC based on rather thin evidence – at least that's what I thought – but there may well be much more to the story."

Alex added, "And Speedie's notion that Flint might be working for an extensive criminal organization might be closer to the mark than we gave him credit for. Maybe Archie Staples will be able to turn up some more for us to work on."

As they turned off the Great North Road to head for Wheathampstead, Angela said, "That confirms my paranoid suspicions about being followed – there's been a big black limousine behind us ever since we cleared the suburbs, and he's just turned off too!"

Alex said, "There is another possible explanation, as well, Angela – he might just be headed for the same place as we are – Harpenden University. Nevertheless, let me check!"

He gave the recommended hand signal for slowing down, and pulled onto the grass verge, whereupon the big car swept past. All they could make out was that it was driven by a uniformed chauffeur, with a peaked cap, and that there were more than a couple of people in the rear compartment.

"Either they're more cunning than us," said Melpomene, "or your suspicions were unfounded – I wouldn't go so far as to accuse you of paranoia – as detectives we tend to think in that sort of way, too!"

"Which has occasionally got us out of tight corners!" added Alex, "Anyway, let's drive on and see if we find anything interesting when we get there."

They parked in front of the administration building as before and decided to walk to Pat's not-so-elegant 'Hall of Residence'.

As they went into the hutment and started to walk towards Pat's room at the end, Angela said, "It looks better inside than out! It wouldn't bother me at all to live in a place like this, if there are any vacancies. Perhaps Pat or one of the others would know."

Pat was in her room, with books and journals spread out in front of her, but she jumped up eagerly, saying, "What a good excuse for a break – tea anyone?"

They all accepted, and while she set off to the tea-room, saying, "I'll bring a tray, if someone will help me with the tea-pot!", Alex wandered over to the window, then whistled and said, "We get a good view of the manor-house from here – come and see what's parked on the drive! I'm sure that's the big car that overtook us on the way here! I'll ask Pat about it when she gets back."

Pat knew immediately, "That's Lord Ellsworth's car – he seems to zoom all over the country in it, attending to his business interests. I believe he's a very wealthy man – he has tripled his inheritance, they say, over glasses of beer down at the Poacher, and his late father was no pauper!"

"What field is he in?" asked Melpomene, "I heard about a Lord last year who was, for a while, a successful confidence trickster in partnership with his lady wife – if you exude an air of nobility or even respectability, you can get away with a great deal, apparently. I hasten to add that I'm not accusing Lord Ellsworth of criminality, but in my book it's not easy to make an enormous fortune and remain completely honest!"

"They say," said Pat, "down at the public bar of the Poacher – which is where I acquire most of my information – that his estates in Nottinghamshire turned out to be right on top of a number of seams of high-quality steaming coal. The Wheathampstead property here doesn't have the same geology, so the experts at the pub tell me!"

"What did the estate look like, before Ellsworth made his gesture of allowing the University to be built on it?" asked Alex.

"Just ordinary grazing land, like so much in this area. Some of the adjacent properties have been turned into golf courses, several of them with hotels which had formerly been manorial residences – again I'm quoting the local experts."

"I can certainly believe in that!" said Melpomene, "I myself grew up in Woodhampton Castle in Hampshire – transformed, after my father passed away, by Lady Cynthia Musgrave, my Mama, into a very successful hotel – no golf course, but tennis courts, some coarse fishing and, in the season, some renowned shooting!"

"So you are really an Honourable!" exclaimed Pat.

"When I feel like wielding a bit of prestige, yes! But I keep that charm very much in reserve, so as not to devalue it! Coming back down to earth, what would be the best way of finding out the source of Lord Ellsworth's wealth?"

"The trouble with asking around at the pub," said Pat, "is that everything there is built on hearsay. When everyone agrees on a notion, then you can feel more secure. As a historian, I'm well aware of the values and drawbacks of common knowledge!"

Chapter 19

"When I telephoned you this morning, Pat," said Melpomene, "you said you had something interesting for us – so what was it? Something else that you'd learned at the pub?"

Pat laughed, "Not this time, Mel! No, this is the product of a bit of sleuthing on campus. You remember Penny, who you met after you'd been watching the girls play tennis? Well she's studying Political Science, and was rather cock-a-hoop at finding a possible skeleton in the cupboard of Sir Desmond Killane, the Deputy Vice-Chancellor – who is not generally liked. She was going through the early history of the foundation of the Labour Party, particularly the influence of the Fabian Society, finding that Killane resigned from it over a controversy over the abolition of hereditary peerages – at that time he was waiting in the wings to inherit his father's baronetcy. But that's not the interesting bit! Penny reckons he owes his present position at this University to the patronage of Lord Ellsworth, after he helped to bring about the downfall of one of Ellsworth's competitors."

"How did he achieve this?" asked Alex, "By violent skullduggery or something more subtle?"

"Merely by exposing his illegal dealings on the Stock Exchange. The man was a mining geologist and had created a sizeable fortune by locating rich ore deposits and keeping the information to himself until he had acquired large parcels of shares in the right companies. This is called insider trading, they tell me, and it's highly illegal!"

"This is all very fascinating, Pat," Melpomene went on, "But has it any direct connection with our own enquiries?"

"It certainly has, Mel and Alex, because neither Ellsworth nor Killane have left it there. From what she's found out, Penny is convinced that the two of them have decided it was too profitable an experience not to be repeated – but you really ought to talk to her – I'm just a fascinated bystander!"

"We certainly will!" said Alex, "Is Penelope on campus at the moment?"

"She said she would come back here as soon as she had finished her session with her supervisor, so she should turn up shortly. Another cup? We might have some chocolate biscuits somewhere, too, as long as Penny hasn't scoffed them all!"

As expected, Penny breezed in while they were chatting over tea. She was whistling and looked quite pleased, "Dr Dennison swallowed all my suggestions about concentrating on the Fabian Society – I kept the stuff about Killane under my hat until I've got a much more complete story, but she told me that the library at LSE has a specialized collection focusing on early Labour Party history, so I shall go down and root about there happily!"

"LSE is my Alma Mater," said Mel, "and if the librarian there is still Mickey Sedgwick, you'll find he is very obliging to students, even postgraduates from other universities. Mention my name and watch the eyes roll!"

"Ah-hah!" said Penny – but Mel quickly said, "Nothing like what you're thinking, the man is old enough to be my father! Now tell us more about dear Sir Desmond and his shenanigans. Pat didn't know all the details."

"Right – are you sitting comfortably? Then I'll begin! Pat mentioned the business about the mining geologist, no doubt? I believe that this was the starting-point for the shifty relationship between Ellsworth and Killane. This began a couple of years ago, but since then I reckon this pair and their minions have gone on to navigate the circles of Danté's inferno, and from the bottom up! They have already traversed the Ninth Circle, Treachery, and the Eighth Circle, Fraud, and I'm worried that soon they will enter the Seventh Circle, Violence, if they have not already done so by way of Finchley Road underground station!"

Both Melpomene and Alex sat up at this remark, Mel asking, "What makes you think there is a connection here, Penny? Or are you just musing?"

"I'll tell you what I've found out, and you can make your mind up. Alex, do you remember talking to our Mr Benson, the first time you visited here? He is the Admissions Manager here – you may also recall that he made an attempt to entice Pat here into his web, by offering her some unspecified advantages, like a research trip to Greece. What I think is that he and his cronies, Killane, and even Lord Ellsworth, became worried that Cyril Speedie was getting too close to finding up what they are up to! We need to investigate further, of course – are you up for it?"

"How did you find out that they suspected Speedie?" asked Mel, "Have you got informants embedded in the organization, or have you been rifling through filing cabinets, or what?"

Penny smiled a mysterious smile, put her hand on Mel's arm and said, "Vot you must realize, mein junge freund, is zat ve are living in a rural area of England, where in every village there are nosy people, with their lives starved of excitement. When any stranger appears on the scene, the gossip starts – and this campus is a prolific source of strangers! If you can form a bond with any of the locals, they will be only too willing to share that gossip with you – you are from a small country town, Melpomene, so you must know this already! Since I have come to trust you two, I will begin tell you the identities of some of my most valuable contacts here."

"I think I can begin to guess some of these, Penny," said Alex, "is the headquarters, perchance, of some of them, the public bar of The Hertfordshire Poacher?"

"Of course it is! – now that was not so difficult, was it? All right, I won't waste any more time on silly guessing games – the situation is too serious for that. My other sources are more specialized, I should say. I am the proud owner of an Austin Seven, being too poor to own a larger car just yet – and it has a small petrol tank, so I often have to visit the local garage, and I've made it my business to become very chummy with the mechanic there, Sid Small. He is my second major source of information, particularly because both Ellsworth and Killane have their cars serviced there – their alternative would be to go to Harpenden. Lord Ellsworth has the chauffeur-driven Daimler limousine that you have already spotted, and Desmond Killane runs a new Wolseley – that I think was bought for him – he had a shabby little Singer when I first came here."

"Anyone would think, listening to you," said Mel, "that you have set out to scrutinize the upper levels of the hierarchy here!"

"Anybody would be dead right, too! It could certainly do with a bit of scrutiny! Fortunately Sid Small is a bit of a Red – and he saw that he had found kindred spirits in me and the other protestors, so he was very forthcoming. One of the first things he disclosed to me 'confidentially' was that Lord Ellsworth runs two sets of accounts with the garage."

Chapter 20

"Why would Ellsworth run two garage accounts?" asked Melpomene, "I suppose, since you have brought it up, that it must be for some nefarious purpose, is that so?"

"I forbore to ask Sid Small for a look at his books," said Penny, "that would have tested our relationship unnecessarily – but I have it in mind to drop some innocent queries into the conversation later. One reason that a business keeps two sets of books is to evade taxes, but I think Ellsworth has a different motive – maybe he's soaking the university for his personal expenses, or something of the sort."

"You could ask your friend Sid if he sends the accounts to different addresses," said Alex, "that might be a clue. And perhaps you could enquire whether his Lordship sends his car and chauffeur specially just to get the tank filled, or calls in while they are on their way somewhere."

"Talking of the chauffeur," said Melpomene, "have you had a chance to talk to him, Penny? Is he a habitué of The Poacher, or does he do his socializing elsewhere?"

"I've never seen him in the public. But there's also another bar, variously referred to as the private bar or the snug, which I've never tried – I'll ask around, shall I? Or maybe you two could, since you are new patrons – it might seem more usual for a couple to prefer somewhere less full of noise and smoke than the public. I do know his name – it's Clive Sturgeon."

"I'm beginning to think we might take up residence in The Poacher for a while," said Alex, "it's earlier than we had planned, but I don't think we'll have much trouble in changing our booking – what do you think, Mel?"

"The only problem is that we'll have to go home first, to get some clothes and washing things – but that won't take us more than about three hours altogether, and we needn't both go! Bags I it's me, Alex – I prefer to make my own choice of things, and you can give me a list of your modest requirements! Better ring the pub first, to make sure they've got a room free."

Because of the earlier experience, as Melpomene turned onto the London road, she glanced in the mirror and saw that a white saloon, a

Morris or an Austin she thought, had turned after her. So she kept an occasional eye on it for a mile or two. Then she saw a side-road with a sign to Hatfield, so swung onto it, as a test. The following car did the same! After a couple of miles, Mel pulled over, got out, and spread a map on the bonnet. The pursuer drove by, but slowed to a crawl, and Mel caught sight of the driver, a woman wearing a cloche hat and furs!

Melpomene quickly got back in, pulled the Riley round in a sharp u-turn and headed back to the main road. Sure enough, the white car followed, and turned onto the main road with her. Mel thought, "Well, I wonder if she's going to be with me all the way back to the flat? I'd better be prepared for any eventuality!" She felt in her handbag, beside her on the seat, to make sure her Beretta was there, loaded as always, and she cocked it and took off the safety.

Sure enough, as she turned the Riley in to the laneway where it was usually parked, the white car went past, driving slowly as though looking to park. Mel got out, with her gun in her side jacket pocket so she could put her hand on it quickly, and went to the front steps of the flat. Before she could go up, the woman in the cloche approached, saying, "Don't be alarmed, my dear, but I urgently need to talk to you privately! My name is Irene Bradshaw."

Melpomene quickly made her mind up and said, "Well, Miss Bradshaw, you had better come in!", led her up to the front door and opened it with her key.

Caroline was a little surprised to see her, so Mel said, as calmly as she could, "Please make us cups of tea, Caroline, or perhaps Miss Bradshaw would prefer coffee? Come and sit down, please, and you can tell me what's on your mind."

When they were comfortable and Caroline had brought a tea-tray and some fruit-cake and left them, Mel looked expectantly at the woman, who began.

"I realize this is all unforgivably rude and unexpected, but I've been getting more and more concerned! But let me start at the beginning – I was engaged as personal assistant to the Deputy Vice-Chancellor, Sir Desmond Killane only a few weeks ago. At first, of course, I was very busy getting acquainted with the administrative systems at Harpenden, and finding out what duties Sir Desmond expected of me, but after a while I began to wonder at some of his activities."

"That's very interesting, Miss Bradshaw – is that why you decided to talk to us?"

"That's right – a student I know, Anthea Talbot, told me you and your husband were investigating irregularities in admission procedures, so I thought that this was an opportunity to look at some of Sir Desmond's other dealings. You should be aware – I think he must have forgotten this although I made no secret of it when I was interviewed – that I am a qualified and experienced accountant and so had no difficulty in seeing when rules were being flouted! Being new and to a degree on probation, I decided not to say anything at the time, but merely resolved not to be drawn into any wrong-doing."

"Were you asked to participate in anything illicit, Miss Bradshaw – or may I call you Irene? Please call me Melpomene or Mel – or were you just waiting for this to arise?"

"That's about the strength of it – but I heard about this dreadful event with Mr Speedie in the tube station, and then overheard Sir Desmond talking about it on the telephone and actually laughing and saying 'Speedy come and Speedy go!' or some similar comment. I quietly closed the door and I don't think he had noticed me coming into the room! That was the moment when I resolved to seek help! I hadn't enough to take it to the police, so I thought of you!"

"And I'm very glad you did, Irene! Do you know who Killane was talking to on the telephone? Did he use a name?"

"Not that I heard, Mel, but I can say he seemed very relaxed – not like someone talking to a superior, nor even to an employee, but more like to a close associate."

"Tell me, Irene, are you going to go back to your office? Will Killane want to know what you've been doing and where you have been? Does he keep tabs on you?"

"Not at all! Apart from my suspicions about him, he is an affable and undemanding employer. Besides, he is off playing golf this afternoon!"

"Ah-hah!" said Mel, "Do you know at which club? My husband Alex is a golf enthusiast – this might open up another line of enquiry and Alex might even be able to establish a social relationship with him – under an assumed name, of course. What a dreadful pun! – *un nom de terrain de golf*! I like it!"

Chapter 21

"Please excuse me for a moment, Irene," said Melpomene, "I'd like to let Alex know where I am and what is going on – as far as he knows I've just come here to pack our bags for a few days away. I'll have to telephone our office first and get the number of Pat Georgiadis' digs."

She rang and said, "Oh hello, Winnie, I'm at the flat picking up some stuff – can you give me the number for our friends the postgraduate students' digs at Harpenden? Thanks for that – I'll fill you and Marjorie in later. Any interesting mail? Not much, that's good – we've decided we'll spend a few days in Harpenden, probably coming back next Tuesday, so if you and Marjorie want to take a couple of days off, you're welcome."

"Now, Irene, pour yourself another cup while I talk to Alex – I'll try to make it short."

Another student answered the telephone, but soon Alex was found, so Melpomene related the events of the morning to him and said she would be back in the late afternoon. Then she turned back to Irene.

"Have you any thoughts about what you'll do next? Speaking as a detective, I would find it potentially very useful to have you as a source close to a member of the conspiracy, but you might feel that this is too dangerous a role to play, and we wouldn't want to put you in a position of risk. What do you think, Irene?"

"Actually, Mel, I feel quite keen! Sir Desmond seems to trust me, and I have access to most of his correspondence, of course. When I first spotted some of his doubtful financial transactions, I held my tongue and just kept notes – I think that this sort of thing alone could be quite valuable for us – listen to me, Mel, I'm saying 'us' already! And he has one of those office telephone setups where I'm on an extension in my next-door office, so that he can buzz me and ask me to get someone, so it would be very easy for me to eavesdrop without him knowing it! I followed you this morning because although he was off playing golf, I didn't want to reveal any connection with your agency, and I don't know who else in the admin departments is in cahoots with him."

"Very wise, Irene, we'll make an operative of you very quickly! What are your plans for the rest of the day – are you driving straight back to the University?"

"No – I already told Killane I would take the opportunity of his break for golf to visit my Mum and Dad – they live in Elstree, so that made a very convenient excuse in case I am in fact being watched."

"Excellent! Do you want to tell me anything else before we part?"

"Only that I've just recalled which golf club Killane belongs to – it's called Doggett Hall – I should have remembered because it's an exclusive club and he's always going on about his membership and the influential contacts he has made over drinks and meals!"

"Great, Irene, but I hope that won't make it too difficult for Alex to play as a visitor there! At least he doesn't give the impression of being an obvious arriviste!"

"I look forward to meeting him, Melpomene. I shall see you back on campus, or even in the Hertfordshire Poacher. I suppose we can contrive some encounter that doesn't look like a prearranged plotters' meeting – Killane himself doesn't seem to go there, but who knows about his confederates!"

After Irene had left, it didn't take long for Mel to throw some clothes and toiletries into a couple of bags. Then she got Mrs Mountain to make her some sandwiches, ate a couple of them with a cup of tea there and then, and took the rest to eat en route.

As she set off, she couldn't help checking in the mirror all the time in case she was being followed, but couldn't see anyone, neither in the suburbs nor when she was on the main road, so decided she was not going to let herself become paranoid. After she had turned off for Wheathampstead she found a place to stop, finished her sandwiches and had some ginger beer from a bottle. She was soon parking outside the main building on campus, got out, and wandered toward the hall of residence, only to find it deserted.

Mel tried the refectory and the student bar, but there was nobody she knew at either, so she asked the student bar-tender if he knew Pat, or Penny or any of that group. "Sorry!" he said, "I've only just come on, ready for the evening. As you can see, the place hasn't started filling up yet – I expect there will be more in an hour or so. Have you tried the tennis courts or the indoor sports hall?"

"I don't even know where that is – but I could see that the tennis courts were not in use as I came by."

He explained where the indoor sports building was, and Melpomene made for it, passing a couple of teaching buildings on her way.

As she pushed open the door, she could hear the sounds of activity and when she went into the main gym she saw that there were several games in full swing – including men's and women's badminton and a netball match. And there in the spectators' seats by the netball court she saw Alex, Pat and several other students, cheering on their teams, among which Mel could see Penny, Anthea and two others from the tennis game which had introduced them on the first visit to the campus, whose names she had forgotten for the moment.

The game was soon over, and the winners were Penny and Anthea's team. After the customary hugs all round, they came over to talk to their fans, now including Mel, who said, "I missed most of the game, but congratulations anyway!"

"Phew!" said Penny, mopping her face, "I could do with a cool drink – shall we get it here, they have a little snack-bar in this building, Mel, or shall we go to the main student bar?"

"Here, I think!" said one of her team-mates, "I would need a shower before I feel presentable enough to appear in public!"

They sat down and chatted while they sipped their drinks, and while Mel wolfed a sausage roll, having already forgotten her rather ladylike cucumber and cottage cheese sandwiches.

"How did you get on?", said Alex quietly. "No problems or further incidents, Alex. I'll tell you the whole story once we can relax at the pub. I trust you had no trouble with the booking?"

"None at all – if we want, we can stay for up to a week, but I told them it probably wouldn't be quite as long. We shall see what eventuates!"

"I'm glad I brought more than one outfit, then. I didn't think you'd need your dinner-jacket here, was that right?"

"That's fine – even if we go to dinner at the Blue Boar!"

Chapter 22

As they were unpacking their bags in the pleasant room they had been given at the pub, Melpomene asked, "Was that just an idle mention of the Blue Boar, Alex, or are you plotting something?"

"Just a half-formed idea," replied Alex, "we were told by someone, maybe it was Pat, that Lord Ellsworth and his cronies are accustomed to dine there on occasion. Apparently it is a fairly high-class restaurant in Harpenden town, but during the week I hardly think that diners would dress – we are in the provinces, don't cha know – so I wouldn't need a dinner-jacket. Of course, that needn't inhibit you from getting glamorous – I assume you've brought something suitable!"

Mel didn't answer, but merely held up a hanger with the long slinky green number that Alex remembered her wearing at some reception or other at the end of a previous case.

"How would we pick an evening when our quarries are dining, Alex? I scarcely think they would be there every night."

"Come, come, my dear, after all, we are detectives! A discreet telephone call to the restaurant management could be devised, I'm sure. But not tonight – let's settle in here first – but we might also make a recce of the snug after dinner. Sir Desmond might even be back from golf and celebrating his round there – or bemoaning the unfortunate or unfair circumstances that cost him extra strokes."

"More likely to be impressing his acquaintances at Dogget Hall, if I read him right!" said Mel. "Do you think you'll be able to parlay your way in there? Irene gave me the impression it's a rather exclusive club."

"She sounds as though she'll be a great asset to us, Mel – I look forward to meeting her – and she can tip us the wink when her boss is planning another day on the course. I think I will telephone Archie Staples – he has a lot of golf cronies in the Bar fraternity, so he might be able to wangle me an invitation to Dogget Hall. At a pinch I could also talk to Monty Petherick – even though I'm perennially dubious about him, he still could be useful for this sort of thing – he's a bit of an operator."

"We can talk about this a bit more over dinner, Alex, I'm feeling ready for it, aren't you?"

The dining room was not yet full, so they picked a table in a position which gave them a good view of the other diners. A waitress took their orders, and Alex suggested that they might try a glass of the house red, which turned out to be remarkably acceptable for such an out-of-the-way establishment.

When they had disposed of the soup, both chose lamb cutlets, and as they enjoyed them, Melpomene brought up the subject of the planned excursion into the snug. When the plates were being taken, she asked the waitress whether it was open to the general public.

"Oh yes, madam, it's called the private bar, but that's just to distinguish it from the public. It's a bit more comfortable and quiet – people play cards there, or even draughts or chess, rather than darts or shove ha'penny, which can get a bit boisterous! If you take coffee, we can serve it there, with liqueurs if you like, unless you have it here with your dessert."

"Thank you for that," said Mel, "we'll both have some of that delicious-looking apple pie I've just seen on the next table, and then we'll take our coffee in the snug."

"That sounds very promising!" said Alex, "We can play a hand of crib or something and scan the other guests at our leisure without any commitment."

They finished their meal and then found their way to the snug. Indeed it gave a very good first impression – there were maybe ten people already there, some just talking together while they enjoyed drinks, some reading newspapers or magazines – Alex saying, "Oh good – I see they have 'Golfers' World', I can have a read of that if there's nothing else happening!" And there were a couple of tables of card-players – what looked like a four of bridge and an elderly pair playing crib.

Melpomene collected cups of coffee at the serving-hatch, which offered a view through to the main public bar, and asked for a pack of cards and a cribbage board. They found a table in the corner and settled down to drink their coffee and try to remember the rules of crib.

"I used to play this all the time when I was young," said Mel, "my grandmother and the aunts were practically addicts – but it has been a while now, so I hope it will come back to me!"

"We could ask that old couple," said Alex, "but that might make us conspicuous, which is the last thing we want!"

Between them, Mel and Alex recalled sufficient of the rules to play an enjoyable couple of games of 121-up, and while they were playing and chatting, looked around at the others in the room. Some people drank up and left, and then four men came in, bearing mugs of beer from the public bar, collected two packs of cards and settled down near Mel and Alex.

"What'll it be tonight, mates?" said one, and another suggested, "How about Solo? We ain't played that or Euchre for a while, 'ave we Clive?", getting the reply, "Don't see why not, Sid, Solo's as good as any!"

Alex looked meaningfully at Mel, who nodded and murmured, "The chauffeur and the garage bloke! We may have struck gold already!"

"My gawd!" said Clive, after the first deal, "A lay-down Misere straight off – must be my night!" and play on that table continued with a certain amount of accompanying banter – but nothing too boisterous. Then, in between hands, another player said, "Been on any long runs lately, Clive? Or is His Lordship staying close to home at present?"

"Strange you should ask, Freddy, I 'ad to take him and a couple of rum-looking types – one of 'em was tall with a big red conk and a little mo, and the other looked like a bank manager or something – to Harwich a few days ago, to put 'em on a ferry to the Hook of Holland. As soon as they was safely on board, Ellsworth pulled out 'is 'ip-flask and swallered the best part of half a pint of brandy – he was trembling like a leaf, but the drink seemed to calm 'im down. By the time I dropped him off home he seemed all right again – gawd alone knows what that was all about!"

Mel stood up at that point and persuaded Alex to leave, too. "I wanted to make sure we were not seen as taking too much interest in that conversation, Alex – you were getting dangerously close to gawking as that story went on! I don't think anyone noticed, but not everyone has the training in social anthropology that I have!"

They waved cheerily to the barman, who was wiping down his counter, went out and ascended the stairs to their room.

Chapter 23

As soon as they were in their room with the door shut, Alex said, "I assume you jumped to the same conclusion as I did – Lord Ellsworth was smuggling the thugs who murdered Cyril Speedie out of the country! The description tallies quite closely with what that kid said at the tube station."

"I agree, Alex, but what his lordship may not have realized is that there is an international police organization being set up at this very moment – I assume you have a number for Sir Adrian Fitz-Hugh in your little book. First thing in the morning we must give him a call, and ask him if he could set his Dutch colleagues onto tracking these two down. We could get onto our contacts in Customs and Excise, too – their Harwich people would likely have a record of all passengers headed for the Hook of Holland."

"The trouble is, Melpomene, that the scent has had a few days to get cold by now – that chauffeur Clive said 'a few days ago', so it's not all that straightforward. Nevertheless, I'm content to leave it in the hands of our professional friends. I'm about ready to have a shower and get to bed – there is a shower here, I trust?"

"Yes, but not in our bedroom, this is only a country pub after all! You have to go along the corridor to get there – it was pointed out when we were shown the room. Fortunately I had the wit to pack dressing-gowns and slippers! Remember that time in Montmartre when we had to drape towels around us and make a dash!"

"How could I forget it, Mel! We could repeat the experience here – as I recall it had a rewarding outcome at the time!"

"Now, now, Mr Crabbe! Restrain yourself for a moment, please!"

After a refreshing night's sleep, Mel and Alex were pleased to find that The Hertfordshire Poacher still clung to English notions of what was a good breakfast, so they tucked into bacon, sausage, scrambled eggs and fried tomatoes with a will, followed by thick brown toast with Rose's Lime Marmalade, and then took their coffee into the snug, where there was a good supply of newspapers, including The Times. Mel asked the waitress whether it would be all right for her to tackle the crossword, and was soon absorbed in solving the cryptic clues, while Alex paged through two or three of the more popular dailies.

Then he sat up with a low whistle and said, "Listen to this, Mel, it sounds as though student unrest is becoming fashionable: *'Exeter, Wednesday: Police were called to the Central Devon Institute this morning when office workers were prevented from entering the Arts and Letters building by a group of young persons, presumably students, standing in a row, with linked arms, across the steps leading up to the main entrance. When the employees asked angrily what was going on, the students did not answer directly, but started chanting incomprehensible words, which a bystander told our reporter were possibly in Latin. A man, later identified as Mr Guy Slocombe, the director of the examinations department, attempted to push past the human barrier, but was simply pushed back. No blows were exchanged, but Mr Slocombe abandoned his efforts and left the scene with a few of his colleagues. When a police car arrived with four officers, the protesters dispersed and indeed vanished, with no argument, and the employees proceeded to their places of work. Mr Slocombe stated that he had no idea what the protest was about, and that nothing like it had occurred there before, to his knowledge.'*

"We'll have to look into this later, Alex, but now you might try to telephone Adrian Fitz-Hugh and see if he can get his international team to leap into action over our fugitive suspects."

Sir Adrian was quite pleased to hear from them, and said he would put someone reliable onto the job, adding, "We'll contact Jimmy Manley, too, and see if he's managed to garner any more information on these assailants – his people have most likely interviewed all the eyewitnesses and possibly tube-station staff also who might have seen anything further – in my opinion he's a very thorough investigator! They tell me you're working on a case at Harpenden University – what's that all about, Alex?"

"How did you hear about that, Adrian?"

"Well, first we put two and two together when we were looking into Mr Speedie's circumstances – and then your secretary, Marjorie, mentioned it when I was making a friendly call to your office yesterday!"

"Yes, I see, no problem. Well the late lamented Cyril Speedie was involved – what we were called in for, though, was to investigate what appeared to be irregularities in enrolment and admission practices at Harpenden – and curiously enough, we have just seen a newspaper report of a student protest in Exeter – we haven't had a chance yet to find out whether there is any connection, or indeed what it was all about. While I think of it, I'll give you the number of the student lodgings here – they know us and would be able to find us when we're on campus. At the moment we're staying at a pub in Wheathampstead, near Harpenden – the Hertfordshire Poacher, so I'll give you that number, too."

"I'll see what we can do to track down those two suspects, Alex," said Adrian, "but I can't say that our chances are very good by now. I'll get onto Customs at Harwich, too. As for establishing links between the protests there and in Exeter, I'm afraid that's out of our line, so we'll have to leave it to you and the local police forces. Have you established your bona fides with the Hertfordshire Constabulary yet? It's a bit far away from Jimmy Manley's patch over there, is it not?"

"Thanks, Adrian – we understand that the trail might have cooled off by now, but we know you will do whatever is possible. I'll get on to Jimmy Manley and see whether he knows anyone in the district – it's always good to work with acquaintances – but if not, I'll get onto the station in Harpenden, since I don't know whether there's one in this place – it's hardly more than a village."

"Find out whether the University has a security officer – they may already have established relationships with the local constabulary. Best of luck, Alex – don't hesitate to telephone me at any time – my best to Melpomene!"

Mel had been listening of course and needed to ask only a couple of questions to confirm small points, and added, "Now, let's head off for the campus and see whether there have been any developments. Perhaps we'd better check with the office first – but Winnie and Marjorie may have taken up our suggestion to take a couple of days off, of course. We'll see, I'll ring now. Oh – 'no answer' was the stern reply!"

So Alex and Mel headed out to get into the Riley. As they passed the reception desk, the attendant said, "While you were on the telephone just now, a young person called in and asked for you – I could see by the switchboard lights that you were talking, so she said she would catch up later – name of Pat."

Chapter 24

As soon as they had parked in their usual spot on campus, Melpomene and Alex went to Pat's room, where they found her and Penny and another two women in earnest discussion.

As they walked in, discreetly tapping on the door to announce their presence, Pat stood up and said, "I'm so glad you got here so quickly – we have a slightly concerning state of affairs developing. Mel and Alex, you know Penny, of course, now meet Olive and Lucy – they have come here on a mission from our other campus, in Harpenden town itself – the School of Architecture."

Mel remembered something, "Didn't Angela Dayton tell us about someone who had been refused entry to that school unless his industrialist uncle directed some of his consulting their way?"

One of the newcomers, Lucy, said, "Would that have been Tristan Hargreaves? We showed him round when he came for his admission interview – I'm on the committee of the Students' Union, and we like to introduce ourselves to prospective students. We knew he had not been admitted, but nobody knew why exactly."

Mel said, "Yes, Lucy, we were told his whole sorry tale – I can fill you in later, when we have a moment. Sorry, Pat – I interrupted you before. What is this matter of concern?"

"No need to apologise, Mel!" Pat said, "We only have suspicions at this stage, but there are signs that the high management here are embarking on a programme of weeding out undesirables. I don't know how it is at other universities, but here postgraduate students like us can usually pick up part-time tutoring appointments – they don't pay much but they're still very useful for those of us who are on scholarships. Even where parents and family are supporting our studies, this income, modest though it is, is very welcome. My parents are not well off, but they've been very good at supplementing my scholarship, and it feels nice to be able to make a contribution myself. Have a look at this – lots of us have been getting these in the last day or two, on the Architecture campus, too!"

Pat handed Mel a single sheet of typescript, and she read it out:

'Memo to: Miss Parthenope Georgiadis, Doctoral Candidate, Faculty of History and Political Science. I am sorry to have to inform you that

this University has been forced to introduce various cost-cutting measures, and consequently, from the beginning of next term, we shall not be able to continue your part-time tutorial fellowship on its existing terms. Please be assured, this does not affect your candidacy for the degree of PhD. If you wish to discuss this further, please make an appointment to see the undersigned. Malcolm North, Assistant to the Bursar.'

Pat went on, "I know of three or four postgrads who got similar letters, and for all I know there were others – we tend to know about people only in our own faculties. Furthermore – and this is getting quite grim – the rot seems to be spreading to the academic staff at lecturer level and even above. My supervisor was engaged in a heated conversation with a colleague when I turned up for one of my regular sessions with him only yesterday. They stopped, mainly in deference to me, I think, but the colleague said, as a parting shot, 'You heard about Tommy Treadwell, I suppose – he's only five or six years off retirement and they've just given him his marching orders, with only a four-weeks notice!' Maybe I'm being paranoid, Mel and Alex, but I'm beginning to think that poor Mr Speedie may have been merely the first in a series of people to be eliminated, one way or another!"

"What I'm wondering about," said Alex, "is who are the plotters here? We have pretty strong evidence that Lord Ellsworth is a villain – maybe even the ringleader – and it's also likely that Sir Desmond Killane is heavily implicated. As for Benson, the admissions officer, he could simply be following orders without actually being part of the plot. We need to find out, as well as seeing who else is involved. We are very fortunate that we have someone in a position to pass us sensitive information – I mention no names at the moment, but Melpomene knows who I mean."

"This brings up the question of our own security," said Mel, "it would be very tempting to share all our information with anyone who appears friendly – those present here today, for example – but this degree of openness has risks. Careless talk could have bad consequences for us – we're dealing, as we have discovered, with evil ruthless people! So please excuse us, ladies, if we seem less than forthcoming on occasions!"

"No need to make excuses!" said Lucy. "I'm sure that this is entirely necessary – but you did say you would tell us more about Tristan Hargreaves."

"Quite right!" said Alex and proceeded to relate the attempt at stand-over tactics that Tristan himself had told Angela and her friends about in the bar of the 'Duke of Buckingham'.

"Tristan was informed of his rejection by the Registrar, as I recall," said Mel, "I wonder whether that gentleman was just passing on a proposition put forward by others, or was he a party to it?"

Alex said, "We are obviously going to need a lot more information about the management structure of the university – we can't assume it resembles what we became used to at University College or at LSE. How could we go about discovering this?"

"We have one friendly insider, as we have said," commented Melpomene, "but this person is a recent appointment and admitted to having to work hard to discover administrative practices here. Nevertheless, it would be worth asking – it's quite possible that a lot was found out that might come in handy for our investigations. And, if we wanted to find out more, nobody would find it strange if more questions of the sort were asked by the same person."

Olive, who had been quiet up to then, looking fascinated as she followed the conversation, spoke up, "I might be able to help here – my sister Gwyneth is the senior telephone operator on this campus, and has made it her business to be familiar with the key people in each of the faculties, teaching departments and administrative sections, so that she can direct enquiries from outside to the most appropriate person. Should I speak to her, or would you prefer me to arrange a meeting at home one evening? We often have bridge nights – but strictly for fun, we don't get as serious as some of the dyed-in-the-wool bridge fiends tend to become – I have heard of marriages breaking up because of problems at the bridge table!"

"Oh please try and set up such a social evening!" said Mel, "And I know what you mean about some of those career bridge experts – I've seen nasty rows breaking out at my Mama's hotel on several occasions!"

Chapter 25

Alex broke in, "Do you and your family live close to here, Olive?"

"Yes, in Harpenden. My sister Gwyneth cycles to work here every day! The switch is open for callers from 8 am, but she gets off at 4 in the afternoon and a man takes over until 7 o'clock when the switch usually closes, except when there is an evening meeting of a faculty board or the Senate, or some other important committee – of course many of their members have to attend to their regular jobs during the day."

"So, Olive," asked Alex, "do you know whether the telephones at the Chancellory go through the university switchboard?"

"Yes, except that I think Lord Ellsworth has some private lines. I'm not absolutely sure about this – I'll ask Gwyneth, or you can when you come to our place. She won't talk about personal matters while she's at her post!"

"We're opening up some promising leads, here!" said Alex, "That reminds me – did you manage to speak to Tony Philpotts, Pat? You thought he might be able to tell us more about some of the people in the administration from an insider's point of view."

"I did manage to catch him, Alex, and he was quite willing to talk – but I don't think he knows much that will be of help to us. His duties mainly seem to be in the areas of equipment purchasing and supplies, and he also takes care of making travel bookings. He has no responsibility for staffing decisions, which are left to the human resources section. I brought up what Mr Benson had said about travel to Greece, and Tony said, 'He was bluffing, Pat, he has nothing to do with such matters – even if he made recommendations, there are committees who actually decide these things on a University-wide basis!' So that, at least was one piece of relevant information!"

"So that was about all you could find out, Pat – a bit disappointing!"

"Wait a mo, Alex, there was something else! As I was leaving, he said 'See you again, Pat – if I'm still here' so I asked him what he meant – was he going to another job or what? And then he said, 'Well, maybe, but not of my own volition! Depends on what the economy drive panel comes up with! They are mainly moving people about and combining departments to save money – that sort of thing. I haven't actually heard of anyone being given the push, but the general rumour is that it will start happening soon!' I had to leave then, because Tony had to see the departmental store man about something that must have been urgent, judging by the body language of the man while he was standing at his door!"

"So you didn't have a chance to ask who was on this economy panel, Pat?"

"No, Alex, but I can make some discreet enquiries – or I could just drop it into the chat at the Poacher next time I see some university people there – there's bound to be opinions and stories floating about! I'll take odds that dear Sir Desmond is involved in some way!"

Olive piped up, "And I'll see if Gwyneth knows anything when I get home tonight! She is usually provided with a list of the chairs of all the committees."

Melpomene was getting a bit nervous, "Pat, have you got any large sheets of paper? I can feel the need to draw a chart growing upon me."

"How about this?" said Pat, reaching up to the top of the wardrobe, "This is cardboard left over from our demonstration banners – it's grey, but that shouldn't matter, should it?"

"Not at all! That'll be perfect! What I want to do is try to get some sense into our lines of enquiry, so we can pursue the important ones ahead of the others. So what I think I'll do is, first of all, start off by listing the sources of information across the top of the sheet, with friendly or neutral ones on the left, graduating across until we get the truly evil ones on the right. Leave me to play for a while, and then we can work on it together. Have you got any coloured pencils or crayons, Pat? Or some soft lead pencils will do at a pinch – we can do several drafts and refine them as we go."

Alex said, "I ought to explain to everyone that Mel is inclined to resort to charts from time to time – it's an approach she picked up in her Social Anthropology studies, and, believe me, it has sometimes paid off!"

Melpomene crouched on the floor with her cardboard, since there was no room on the desk, and set to, amid a great deal of muttering, while the others just chatted over fresh cups of tea.

Then they heard the telephone ringing down the hall, and Penny went out to see whether anyone had picked it up. A girl who had it in her hand saw her and said, "They're asking for Mel or Alex – do you know who they mean?" so Penny fetched Alex, since Mel was still busy.

It was Winnie, saying, "Marjorie and I took Melpomene at her word, so we've taken a day or two off – but I thought I'd better drop in and check the mail, and I'm glad I did! Apart from the usual boring stuff, there was a big buff envelope addressed to you, Alex, from Mr Archibald Staples, KC! I'll read you the covering letter – there was a batch of papers too."

"Go ahead, Winnie, I'm all ears!"

"This is what he says: *'Dear Alex, As I told you, I think, it turns out that Daniel Flint KC is a member of my chambers. I approached our chambers clerk, Ron Bisley in a very off-hand way and asked a couple of innocuous questions, like how long had Flint been using the facilities and that sort of thing – but it soon became obvious that he had rubbed Ron's feathers up the wrong way. Being of a devious turn of mind, I decided to see whether I could take advantage of this attitude, so I offered to buy Ron a coffee and started pumping him about Flint's cases. This opened up the flood-gates, as you will see from the enclosed documents – Ron was obviously dying to talk to someone respectable about what he saw as behaviour that would reflect very badly on the chambers if it ever came out. Like most chambers clerks, Ron has a strong protective sense toward his people – and he has decided that Flint is beyond the pale!'* There is more, Alex, but I guess it's better read along with the enclosures – do you want me to send this to you, or can it wait until you get back?"

"Oh, hang on to it, Winnie, we'll only be here a couple more days. Thank you very much for checking the mail – this was over and above the call of duty and, once again, it reminds us what a wonderful pair of secretaries we have in you and Marjorie!"

Alex went back to Pat's room and gave them all a quick summary, and then had a look at Mel's chart, to which she quickly added a thickly-bordered box entitled 'Daniel Flint' – on the right-hand edge of the sheet, next to a similar one labelled 'Desmond Killane'!

Chapter 26

After a while, Melpomene got to her feet and said, "I can't say that my chart is much more than just a preliminary version, but it has given me one idea at least! The most important lead that we have, the one we need to concentrate on first, seems to me to be tracking down the murderers of Cyril Speedie – and I'm not just talking about the two thugs who pushed him to his death, whom we shall just have to leave to our international police colleagues to find if they can – but those who plotted and arranged this."

"You're right, Mel," said Alex, "let's sum up what we know. All we can say so far is that we have information that Lord Ellsworth was the one who smuggled them out of the country, but that doesn't necessarily mean that he was the brains behind the conspiracy, although he must have taken an active part in it. I think we can believe what the chauffeur, Clive Sturgeon, told his mates over cards – he would have no reason to lie, or even to big-note himself that way."

Mel added, "And we can assume that Sir Desmond Killane is part of the gang, since Irene Bradshaw overheard him chuckling about the demise of Speedie – in a particularly callous way, I might add! It's a pity that Irene didn't know who he was talking to that time, but when she does some more eavesdropping she might pick up further ideas. I formed the impression that she has her wits about her, so I hope she takes steps not to get rumbled!"

"And as for why these villains decided that Speedie needed to be eliminated, we can only guess," said Alex, "we know already that he had been investigating various cases of Daniel Flint KC – and when we get back to the office we shall find out what else Archie has turned up about him – but what threat this presented to Ellsworth and his associates we have yet to discover. It must have been serious to drive them to murder!"

"I've been trying to remember whether Cyril Speedie told us about anything else when he was at our office," said Melpomene, "fortunately, at the time, I got Marjorie to take shorthand notes of his conversation with us, so we'll be able to check. Knowing Marjorie, she will have typed them up in a useful form – and she knows never to add anything in these cases, so we will be able to see if he said anything about anybody apart from Flint KC himself. And there are other people whose names I have listed on my chart simply because they have come up – with no real idea whether they are involved in ill-doing or not."

"Who are these, Mel?" asked Alex, "Do you intend to follow them up at all – you must have some reason for including them, surely?"

"Well. I'll go through some of them and make remarks as I go. There's Tony Philpotts, Pat's admin friend – even though Pat didn't get much from him, he's still a potential source of information. Then there's Mark Callaghan, Angela's prospective supervisor and there's Penny's supervisor, too, Dr Dennison, didn't you say, Pen? I've just listed them, not as suspects, but because they probably know a lot about what's going on here."

She went on, "Then there's a group of people who've behaved somewhat suspiciously, such as the smooth Mr Benson, the admissions officer, who tried to persuade Pat to spy for him, and the registrar – don't know his name – who wanted Tristan Hargreaves to get his uncle to send work to the architecture school. Any other grubby persons like that?"

"Not that we've come across so far, anyway!" said Alex, "Archie's files might give us some more leads, with any luck! And we shouldn't forget Irene Bradshaw and Olive's sister Gwyneth – they are potentially valuable sources of information. But now, ladies and gentleman, since we've had only a snack or two all day, I must take my good wife away to seek sustenance at the Hertfordshire Poacher!"

"What of the morrow?" asked Pat, "Do we need to meet again yet – however fascinating this all may be, I have some serious study and writing to do."

"Of course!" said Mel, "Let's make tomorrow a lay-day as far as discussion goes – you ladies have been very good contributors to our investigation, but we mustn't strain your generosity!"

"Before we break up," said Olive, "should I try and arrange for you two to come to dinner at our place, maybe tomorrow evening, to meet Gwyneth and maybe even to play cards?"

"Sounds very good!" said Melpomene, "Let's make the Poacher our headquarters and message centre, shall we? We can leave word there if we decide to go off anywhere."

After freshening up and having quiet cups of tea in their room, Mel finished the crossword she had started before, saying, "I was puzzling and puzzling over this last clue, but now I pick up the paper after doing other things, the answer jumps out at me! This is how detection works sometimes, too, so maybe we'll suddenly get insights about what has been holding us up after we've had a meal and a good night's sleep. Are you ready for dinner, Alex?"

The dining room was more crowded than on the previous evening, and Mel and Alex were shown to a table in the middle of the room, making it a little more difficult to observe others without seeming too obvious, but they still tried.

After disposing of the celery soup – not one of Alex' favourites, they chose a game pie, which the waitress recommended, saying, "There was a shoot over Lord Ellsworth's land a couple of days ago, and they got such a good bag that they passed over some of the birds to us! They've been well hung now, so I hope you'll enjoy it!"

Mel said, "I thought that the estate was all occupied by the university now, isn't that the case?"

"No, madam, there are still lots of woods that the University couldn't make use of, so the shooting is let out. I believe that the group the other day were mainly legal gentlemen. They came here in the evening, and were singing so loudly in the snug that we had to ask them to tone it down for the sake of the other customers. I believe that one of them had an intense argument over this with Mr Piddock, the landlord, but they left, grumbling, after a while!"

Alex and Mel tucked into the meal, which was indeed delicious, then Melpomene said, "You know, Alex, that argument intrigues me – who were these 'legal gentlemen'? I wonder how I can question Mr Piddock about it without being rude?"

"Oh, you'll think of a way of bringing it up, I'm sure, my pet. All you have to do is flutter your eyelashes and you'll have him eating out of your hand!"

"Pshaw!" said Melpomene, "I'll do it my way, thanks very much!"

Chapter 27

"Shall we have dessert?" asked Alex, "I don't know about you, but I found that pie rather filling! I noticed that they have plates of petits-fours in the snug to have with coffee, so perhaps they would suffice."

Melpomene agreed, so they went to the snug, collecting a cribbage-board and cards on the way, and finding a table which would give them a good view of the other guests. When the coffees they had ordered were brought to the table, the waitress said, "Excuse me, but that couple over there – the lady in white with the military-looking gentleman – asked me to find out whether you were bridge-players, because they are short of someone to play with. They said they didn't want to approach you directly for fear you might take offence!"

Alex said, "What do you say, Mel?" and when she nodded, he got up and walked over to the couple. He exchanged a couple of words with them, and then led them back to the table to introduce them to Melpomene, saying, "Please meet my wife, Melpomene. Mel, may I introduce Colonel and Mrs Stavely-Roper – I've explained that we don't consider ourselves top-rank bridge players but are willing to give them a decent-enough game!"

"Of course, dear," said Mel, "we're only too glad – cribbage is a pastime rather than a serious game, I think!"

Mrs Stavely-Roper shook hands with her, saying, "Please call me Felicity, and my husband answers to Randolph when he is in a good mood!" The Colonel bowed and kissed Melpomene's hand, before they took their places, opposite one another.

Their new acquaintances were very affable and easy to talk to, and, to the Crabbes' relief were not obsessed with the game, so they all settled down to an enjoyable few hands, punctuated by further coffees and liqueurs, which the Colonel insisted were his treat.

After a while, the inevitable questions were asked about professions and occupations. Alex said that he was a London solicitor in a small way of business, while Mel was wondering whether she would pursue further studies in her field of social anthropology, hence the present visit to Harpenden University.

Felicity admitted that she was devoted only to working on the committees of various charitable bodies, including one which provided scholarships to assist students from families of modest means, but that Randolph, as well as carrying on a successful agency dealing in commercial property, had on the strength of his Army experience been invited to take a seat on the University Senate. "We only meet four times a year," he explained, "and I shall be joining my colleagues in our next meeting for a couple of days, starting tomorrow."

"Tell me, Colonel," said Melpomene, "what level of decisions does the Senate concern itself with? When I was a student at LSE, I never had any idea what the Senate did – nor the Professorial Board for that matter. I did know a bit about the Anthropology and Sociology Faculty Board – for my sins I was the student rep one term, and I recall we did an awful lot of talking about disputes over exam results and that sort of thing – much too mundane for those higher bodies, I suppose."

"Oh, occasionally we have to deal with minutiae – call me Randolph, by the way, but please not Randy, I beseech you! – I have had only a quick scan through the agenda, which I was sent a week ago, and I did notice a couple of items that dealt with student matters, such as admission criteria, and the like. The major item, however, seemed to be consideration of the report of the Economy Drive Panel, whatever that may be. It is a bit annoying that we haven't yet seen this report – I suppose they are going to table it at the meeting. We shall see!"

The bridge-playing proceeded without serious problems, although Mel had to be reminded of the bidding conventions a couple of times – but their new friends did not make a fuss over this at all. As Mel remarked to Alex later, this was a useful practice session, since Olive's family might well turn out to be sticklers for bridge rules when they met them the next evening.

The topic of the Senate meeting was carefully avoided by Mel and Alex, even though it would have been tempting. The conversation ranged over the Colonel's military experiences, which, as he freely admitted, were largely conducted from Whitehall, with only a brief spell towards the end of the war at a base depot at Le Havre, as he had been assigned to the Royal Army Service Corps. As they got up from the table to retire to their bedrooms, Felicity said, "Oh, that was a very nice evening – could you bear to repeat the experience tomorrow?"

"I'm sorry," said Mel, "we have another social engagement tomorrow evening, but it is an appealing idea – will you still be here in the pub the evening after that?"

"Oh yes," said Randolph, "the meeting is likely to take two whole days, and we don't like driving after dark particularly. So can we look forward to seeing you that evening? I shall probably welcome some activity as a relief from all that talking!"

Back in their bedroom, Alex said, "Excellent! That will give us a chance to get some idea of how the Senate meeting went – who knows what we might learn! I could barely hold my tongue when the subject of the Economy Drive Panel came up!"

"So what shall we do during the day tomorrow, Alex? We can't afford to waste the opportunity of being on the spot, can we?"

"Let's have another look at your chart, Mel. There may be some enquiries apart from those which are already in train. Let me see …"

After a few moments, Alex pointed to an item on the chart and said, "We could try to set up a meeting with Irene Bradshaw, Mel, preferably off campus, I suppose. Why don't we telephone her in the morning – we can be pretty sure that Sir Desmond will be at the Senate meeting, as he's the Deputy Vice-Chancellor, so she'll probably be available, unless he takes her along to meetings, that is!"

"We'll find that out, no doubt, when we try to telephone her, Alex, but I'll give you odds that she is not admitted to sensitive meetings, like this one is bound to be, since she's a comparatively recent appointment and so her loyalties have yet to be established. Also, they probably have minutes secretaries in attendance, so she will not really have any part to play."

"Right, Melpomene! Unless you have any other ideas, that's what we'll do. Now I feel ready for bed – do you want to be first in the bathroom, or can I go ahead?"

"You go, my sweet – I'm going to pop down and get a cup of chocolate – would you like one, too? I don't think this pub runs to room service, and anyway, I think I can manage a small tray."

"See if they have some nice biscuits, too, Mel – those petits fours are but a dim memory by now."

Chapter 28

After another substantial breakfast – this time centred on porridge followed by kippers, for a change – Melpomene and Alex returned to their room to make some telephone calls.

"I'll try the office first," said Mel, "on the off-chance our secretaries are being zealous once again. Oh, nice to hear your voice, Marjorie, can't you bear not being at work?"

Marjorie explained that, after talking to Winnie, she had decided to follow her example and pop in to check the mail.

"But this time I drew a blank – nothing but a council rates demand, not due until next month, and another offer of a Readers' Digest subscription, this time enclosing a sample copy. My doctor has it in his waiting-room so I thought that was enough – and I don't think it will be of much use to the investigation profession! Oh, hang on, Mel, the other telephone is ringing. I'll answer it and get back to you – are you still at the pub?"

When Mel relayed this to Alex he said, "It was Jimmy Manley, at a guess! Better hang on until she rings back and tells us."

And, in less than five minutes, the telephone rang again. Mel picked it up and said, "Hello Marjorie, who was it?" but was answered by Jimmy himself, who said, "She gave me your number, so that'll save a few minutes. What I was ringing about was some information arising from the tube station incident that we've been following up. We spoke to a woman who had complained at the station about being almost knocked over as she reached the street. The stationmaster who dealt with her complaint had the nous to make full notes and pass them on to the local police, who then contacted me. You might be somewhat interested, Melpomene, so I've had it all typed up for you. Meanwhile I'll give you the gist, since you are probably wondering what I'm bleating on about!"

"I was, rather, Jimmy – please don't keep me in suspense!"

"As I said, the woman, Mrs Moira Greensleeves, was almost barged over by two men running from the station, one tall with a moustache – she said nothing about his nose – and another in a suit. She tried to remonstrate with them, but they jumped into a big maroon-coloured car that was waiting there with the engine running and immediately sped off, weaving dangerously through the traffic, she said. But the dear soul managed to see the number plate – at least the letters part, 'VO' and four numbers starting with a '7', she thought. This is a Nottinghamshire number, we looked it up – of course, there are a thousand numbers starting with a '7'. "

"That sounds as though she was unusually observant!" said Mel, "Many witness statements are completely muddled and vague!"

"I can explain that, I think," said Jimmy, "I spoke to Mrs Greensleeves myself, and she told me that she is a loss adjuster working for one of the big car insurance companies, so she's used to being pernickety about details – and when I asked about the make she remembered it was a Lagonda! So I've sent Cec Thomson off by train to visit the Nottingham registration office and see if they can come up with any significant results. I expect to hear from him later today – of course, I'll let you know as soon as we find anything."

"Thanks for that, Jimmy – it would be very handy if we were to find that car registered to any of our suspects. We know Lord Ellsworth has a big black car – but he might have a maroon one as well, of course. See you later, Jimmy, we're now going to discover whether Irene Bradshaw has got anything for us."

Melpomene rang the University, and when a woman answered said, "Hello, is that Gwyneth? This is Melpomene Crabbe. Has your sister Olive told you that Alex and I will be visiting you this evening? That's good, I look forward to meeting you and picking your brains! Meanwhile, can you get Irene Bradshaw for me, please? I've assumed she won't have accompanied Sir Desmond to the Senate meeting. By the way, where do they meet, in the manor house cum Chancellory? Ah, I guessed right – thanks, Gwyneth."

Irene sounded very pleased when Mel rang, but said, "We need to think of somewhere safe to meet. I'd have you here in my room, but you'd have to pass by a number of offices on the way, and who knows which of their occupants are safe! And I would be nervous of being seen in public places, like the refec or the pub, for similar reasons!"

"How about a coffee shop or something similar in another town?" said Mel, "We would have to be extremely unlucky to be spotted in a place like that, and we could pretend to be chance acquaintances anyway – what do you say? We've got our own cars and if we were really paranoid we could keep a watch out for following vehicles."

"Are you pulling my leg, Melpomene? That would be fine. I know a nice little tea-shop in the next village – the Mulberry Bush in Sandridge. If you continue along the road you took to get here from the Great North Road, you'll see a sign to the village on your right, and the tea-shop is near the church, quite easy to find – and, of course, anyone will direct you. Would ten o'clock be too early for you?"

"Terrific, Irene – see you there!"

As she had promised, it was easy to find The Mulberry Bush, particularly because Mel recognised Irene's car parked outside, so they pulled up just as St Leonard's church clock was striking ten. Inside they found that Irene was the only customer, and Mel introduced her to Alex. She was wearing a wide-brimmed straw hat instead of her London cloche, and a tweed skirt and heavy brogues, much more suited to the country.

They settled down in a booth with a view out of the window, and ordered tea and cakes. Then Irene opened her brief-case and took out a thick folder of papers.

"You can look at these as much as you like, and if you want me to copy anything, just make a little mark on the bottom corner – but I've got to smuggle them all back today, before Sir Desmond comes back to his office. I'll talk you through them if necessary and you can decide which are worth copying."

Alex whistled quietly as he leafed through the papers, "Are you sure you've never worked for the Secret Service, Irene? This stuff looks inflammatory – correct me if I'm wrong, but these look like records of orders and invoices for major items for the whole University. Let me show you these two pages – they both list the same items – typing paper, foolscap, 120 reams; ditto, quarto letter-heads, 250 reams and so on, but the prices and payments on the first copy are as much as two to four times those on the second. You are the accountant, Irene, am I jumping to conclusions or what? At first glance, I would guess that one set reflects the truth and the other is for the auditors – am I right?"

"You've hit the nail on the head, Alex – my conclusions precisely!"

Chapter 29

Alex continued leafing through the documents Irene had brought.

"What have we here?" he said, "A bundle of memoranda and notes signed with initials only. Let's see – 'E', I suppose that's Lord Ellsworth – and who would 'MM' be, Irene?"

"That's the Vice Chancellor, Malcolm McArthur, and the other one you might come across is 'HH', the Bursar, Henry Hanson, but I don't know whether any of his notes is in that lot. I have stapled Desmond's replies to each one, whenever he replied in writing, but sometimes he just telephones."

"This is all very interesting and valuable, Irene – there actually is one from the Bursar that is particularly so – I'll read it out, for Melpomene's benefit. *'Desmond: As we decided last week, I will process your 'B' invoices myself, and keep them in my personal file. You will not, therefore, receive the usual acknowledgement from my staff. Be assured that they have been taken care of by me. HH'.* And Sir Desmond just keeps this potentially dangerous stuff in his open files, Irene?"

"Well – not quite, Alex – he thinks they're safely under lock and key, but what he doesn't know is that all the filing cabinets in his office and in mine open with the same key! That's what happens when this penny-pinching University tries to save money by buying job lots of furniture! I found it out accidentally but somehow I forgot to tell him about it!"

"And I suppose you are not ashamed of that either!" said Melpomene, "What else have you got there, Alex? Instructions for eliminating undesirable staff members, or what?"

"Not quite, Mel, but listen to this: *'Sir Desmond: I have invited Lord and Lady Furlong for dinner at the Blue Boar, on Wednesday next week. Apparently Lady Furlong wishes to appraise the cuisine at the Boar with a view to entertaining next month some wealthy friends from the continent who have expressed a desire to experience authentic English regional cooking. We should be delighted if you and your lady would consent to join us and the Furlongs there – 7.30 pm for 8, no need to dress. By the way, you and I have had dealings with these friends before – you will recall the circumstances if I mention*

Lisbon. E.' Very mysterious! I didn't know that this area even had a regional cuisine – did you, Mel or Irene?"

"I would just have thought of it as plain country fare – but I'm no gastronome!" said Mel, while Irene shook her head, too. "It makes me think we should see about trying it out ourselves! Maybe next Wednesday evening would be good, even though we'll have to drive up from London! We should book a table in good time. They don't have a private dining room at the Blue Boar, do they Irene – that would spoil our fun! Of course we don't know whether these Furlongs, or indeed their mysterious friends from Lisbon, are on the side of good or evil!"

"Before we go off on flights of fancy, Mel, let's see what other material Irene has risked her job to bring us. What are these pages here, Irene? They look as though they've been torn out of a record book."

"Right again, Alex – they have been removed by Desmond from the minutes book that is kept of all his dealings with University departments. I am currently responsible for keeping it up, but since I have been in post there have only been two rather low-key meetings, one with the head of the buildings and grounds department and another with the superintendent of the porters and watchmen. I don't really know for certain, but my current belief is that the detached pages contain stuff that Sir Desmond would prefer not to be seen by all and sundry. See what you think – it often takes a fresh eye to spot suspicious passages."

Said Alex, "It looks as though we need to spend some concentrated time on these if we're to get them back safely before Desmond get back. Do you know how long the Senate sessions will run, Irene?"

"The talking will go on until about six today, and there is a dinner arranged for later, but there's a chance that Desmond might go back to his office in between, so I would like to return all this stuff before half-past five, to be on the safe side, Alex."

At that moment, the waitress brought a fresh pot of tea to the table – they had already disposed of two earlier, so Melpomene asked whether they had a lunch menu.

"Not really, Madam, we mainly cater here for people who want teas and coffees and cakes. We can do sandwiches, but nothing substantial. Most people go to one or other of the two pubs here for lunch – the

Ducks and Drakes does traditional ploughman's lunches and cold pork pies, that sort of thing – but if you want a proper sit-down lunch, you should try the Prince of Wales – I went there with my boyfriend on my day off last week and it was very nice!"

"Thanks very much for that! We'll finish our teas and we'll try that one. Is it within walking distance?"

"Oh yes, Madam, it'll only take two or three minutes, so there's no need to move your cars."

So they finished their tea and the last couple of fairy cakes, gathered up the documents and went in the direction the waitress had indicated.

Apparently the Prince of Wales was beginning to fill up, but there were still vacant tables in the dining room. Alex asked the waiter if they could have a table for six, as they were expecting friends – but when Mel flashed an enquiring glance, said quietly to her that he just wanted plenty of table space for the papers!

They took their seats, accepted aperitifs and scrutinized the menu, which indeed looked promising. On the waiter's recommendation, they decided all round on poached turbot, to be followed by Wiener Schnitzel.

Alex said he would take the pages from the minutes book to start with, and suggested that Mel and Irene put their heads together over the correspondence.

"The duplicate invoices can be kept in reserve until they are wanted as evidence when these villains are brought to trial!" said Alex, "But maybe you can gradually accumulate some copies as you go, Irene, and tuck them away somewhere safe!"

Everything went quiet, as perusal of the documents was fitted in between enjoyment of the food, which was certainly of an above-average quality for a country pub. At the end of the meal, only Melpomene opted for apple slice with ice-cream, but everyone took coffee. By this time, the dining room was nearly full, and the waiter was hovering nervously, so Alex asked him,

"Is there a nice lounge bar where we can take this work – we need more time on it, or we'll get stick from the boss!"

"Oh yes, Sir – that door leads to what we call the ladies' bar – but an accompanied gentleman will be quite acceptable!"

Chapter 30

The ladies' bar had comfortable settees, with low tables, so they organized themselves quickly. Irene produced a shorthand pad that she had remembered to put in her bag, so Alex didn't have to squeeze all his notes into the pocket notebook that went everywhere with him.

More coffee was brought, and they were soon working their way through their piles of documents. At first, the three were the only occupants of the room, but after twenty minutes or so a pair of respectable-looking elderly ladies settled in the corner and chatted quietly over their coffee and knitting. After that, others drifted in in twos and threes, until the room was half full, mainly of ladies, one or two of whom glanced pointedly at Alex – nobody said anything, however.

Finally, Melpomene saw that it was nearly four o'clock, so they decided that they would have to leave it at that. Alex said, "I'm pretty happy with what I could get down, so if Irene can make some copies of the papers that we've marked, I think we've done well today! Anyone fancy one for the road? No? Quite wise!"

As they were walking back to the Mulberry Tree to get their cars, Mel suddenly grabbed Alex' arm and pointed. There, parked over the road from the pub, was a big maroon Lagonda, with the number VO 7721!

"You two go back to the car, Alex, and I'll join you in a moment," she said, "don't worry, I'm just going to have a quick look round!"

She went back into the pub, approached the barman and said, "Sorry to bother you, but I think I might have left my fountain-pen behind when we went to the ladies' lounge – I don't want to lose it, it's a rather good Mont Blanc. Has it been handed in?"

"I'll go and enquire, madam, just a moment." He disappeared and while she was waiting, Mel idly surveyed the clientele in the dining room, which had thinned out by now. But there was a table with two largish men in suits, drinking beer and picking at potato crisps, arguing about something, but quite quietly. Melpomene couldn't resist the opportunity to draw on her lip-reading skills, even though one of the men had his back to her, and managed to pick up a few phrases before the barman came back, shaking his head, "If your pen turns up, madam, we'll put it aside for you – your name, please?"

"Henrietta Musgrave. I'll drop in to check next time I'm in the district – thanks for taking the trouble!"

Back at the cars, Alex and Irene were talking and Melpomene told them what had happened.

"I was able to lip-read one of them a little but he started to look at me, so I left. What he said, I think, was 'His lordship will want to know more'n that!' and 'Jesus, Arthur – watch it for gawd's sake!' He was big and burly, with thinning red hair, and his companion, as much as I could see, was thinner and grey. They were both in suits – straight off the rack at Montague Burton's, I should say!"

"Well," said Alex, "as soon as we can, we must let Jimmy know the full registration number – although Cec Thomson might well have come up with it already, he's very good at these sorts of searches. Better get back to your office, Irene, and let's hope that Desmond hasn't dropped in early!"

"I'm not too worried, Alex, and in any case I left the filing cabinet locked and the files in apple-pie order, so he would only notice if he were looking for something I'd pinched. See you both later – I'll telephone you or leave a message for you at the Poacher, one way or the other – and thank you for infusing my dull life with a little excitement!"

Irene got into her car and drove off, and Alex said, "Let's wait a bit, Mel, we really don't want to be seen with Irene on campus, but I would have liked to check in with Pat today, so we can keep each other up to date – maybe tomorrow will do. When are we due at Olive's place tonight? We ought to get there in plenty of time, because Olive is the only one of the family who we've met so far. Should we take a bottle of wine, do you think?"

Back at the pub, Alex tried to telephone Jimmy, but was told that DI Manley was out on a job. "What about DC Thomson? Is he back from Nottingham yet? – OK, I'll try again in the morning. Thanks."

They went up to get ready, have cups of tea and read the papers – the Times and the local paper, the Welwyn and St. Albans Monitor, neither of which held anything of particular interest.

Melpomene parked the Riley in front of the house at ten minutes to seven, and they were let in by Olive, who had been expecting them. She took them to meet the family in the drawing room – Gwyneth, a cheerful blonde woman, a few years older than Olive, and Mr and Mrs

Fletcher, Graham and Clarissa, who welcomed them, gratefully accepted the bottle of Krug champagne, protesting politely that 'they shouldn't have' and made them comfortable with glasses of sherry and some friendly chit-chat.

Olive had obviously been putting the rest of the family in the picture about Mel and Alex' activities, and it was Graham who broached the subject and wished them luck with their enquiries, saying, "I don't think there's too much to worry about with the teaching staff, from what Olive and her friends have told me – it's the admin people who are causing difficulties. By the way, I'm in wholesale groceries, so I do have some business with both divisions of the University – the architects here in Harpenden and also the main Wheathampstead campus. I've had no problems myself, but a couple of people I know on the local chamber of commerce have had disputes over orders from time to time. I can give you their names if you think it's relevant."

"The mention of names," said Melpomene, "reminds me that we were very interested to hear that Gwyneth has made efforts to learn the names and positions of people all over the university, so she can direct telephone calls efficiency. Is this all kept in your head, Gwyneth, or do you have lists?"

"Oh, yes I have, Melpomene, and I've made you a copy of the latest version. It's only a rough typescript and I'm afraid I've scribbled notes all over it, but it might be better than nothing. The public relations office has been promising a proper telephone directory for ages, but I can't afford to wait for them!"

"That's interesting!" said Alex, "Is this public relations office an honest body, or is it a tool of the clique that seems to run this place?"

"Hard to say, Alex, but my own dealings with Madeleine Stone, the PR officer, have always been pleasant. She was a journalist on a big Manchester paper and seems a no-nonsense lady."

Chapter 31

Melpomene had a question for Gwyneth, "I know you like to conduct your work to a high professional standard – does this mean that you avoid any thought of eavesdropping?"

"Yes, of course – that would be completely unacceptable. I usually listen to the first few words, to make sure that I've made the right connection, but then I flip that switch back to the silent position. My switchboard can only manage ten simultaneous calls, after that new callers would get an engaged tone until someone rings off. There are lights to show which lines are in use – I can give you a guided tour if you want, Mel!"

"A further technical question, Gwyneth, before we stop boring the others and turn to some more enjoyable topics of conversation – do you keep a log of inward and outward calls?"

"To the extent that I can, yes I do, but of course I mostly have no way of knowing where an outside call is coming from, only the person or extension they are calling. Sometimes callers tell me their name, so I can pass it on to whoever they are calling, and in those cases I do make a note of that."

At that point, a maid appeared at the door and announced that dinner was ready, so Graham and Clarissa took the arms of Mel and Alex and led them to their seats in the dining-room.

The meal was delicious and was complemented by the Krug champagne and, to finish, some of Graham Fletcher's old tawny port served with cheese and muscatels. Then Clarissa said, "With such a small party, there is no point in having the ladies retire separately from the menfolk, so let's all go back to the drawing-room. Perhaps I can persuade Olive and Gwyneth to entertain us with a song, to Gwyneth's piano accompaniment – could you please, girls?"

"Try and stop us, Mother!" said Olive, "We've recently been practicing some duets, inspired by a concert we went to at the Queen's Hall a couple of months ago, including *'I Would That My Love'*, by Mendelssohn, which is truly beautiful – at least it was when performed by Dora Labette and Muriel Brunskill! But Gwyneth and I will have a crack at it, nevertheless!"

Melpomene said, "Please go ahead – you have to fear no criticism from Alex and me – when we hum along to the wireless it's enough to turn the milk!"

Of course, after a slightly nervous start, the sisters gave a thoroughly respectable performance, Olive's translucent soprano blending perfectly with Gwyneth's rich contralto. Clarissa clapped enthusiastically, saying "That's the value of having a Welsh heritage – what a pity your grandmother is no longer with us to hear you sing so beautifully!"

"Encore, encore!" cried Alex, and the listeners were rewarded by a rendering of *The Flower Duet,* from Lakmé, by Delibes, which Olive apologised for, "We've only just started working on that, and it is very subtle!"

"Oh, don't give up!" said Melpomene, "You two have an impressive talent, even if you might never use it professionally! Alex and I have no artistic pretensions whatsoever, we merely concentrate on fighting the forces of evil!"

"And I'm just a grocer!" said Graham, "But Clarissa is too modest to mention that she's an accomplished water-colourist!"

"Oh!" said Mel, "We had a case a while back which centred on a disputed aquarelle, so we found out a little about the various fields of art. I must say that our work does sometimes have its compensations. Would you show us some of your work, Clarissa?"

They were all taken into Clarissa's studio, which had been a garden room. She hastily threw a cloth over the easel holding her current piece, saying "Not ready for display yet!" and waved to some pictures hung along the back wall.

Mel said, "I was expecting the usual landscapes that amateurs start with, but you have progressed past the apprentice stage, Clarissa – still lifes, portraits and even a nude! She has her face averted, so I won't try to guess the model!"

"I'm not shy – its me!" said Olive, quite proudly, "Mummy has made me look much more beautiful than I really am!"

Alex had been scanning all the pictures and said, "As Mel said, we had a case involving art-works a while back, so we went to a number of auctions, so, although I'm no expert, I would say these would stand up well and sell for substantial amounts if you cared to put them up for sale! Do you agree, Mel?"

"Certainly!" said Melpomene, "We could introduce you to a couple of dealers whom we trust, if you are interested. But we don't want to put pressure on you – perhaps you paint to enjoy it rather than to sell your work."

Clarissa seemed rather overcome with embarrassment, so Graham suggested they return to the drawing room and change the subject.

Alex seized on this, "You mentioned a friend at the chamber of commerce, Graham, who had experienced some difficulties dealing with the university. Can you tell us more – or even introduce us to him if you think that would be acceptable?"

"I'm sure he wouldn't mind talking about it," said Graham, "he certainly complained quite a lot over the drinks and snacks that we usually have following the meetings. I don't remember all the details, but as I recall it his main objection was to do with quantities ordered which were agreed upon and then changed before delivery. His name is Charlie Greengrass, of Stevenage Stationers – they deal with all sorts of paper, notebooks and envelopes, those sorts of things. As well as supplying the university itself they also deal with the Student Union bookshop and various places in Harpenden town."

"I suppose their number is in the book," said Alex, "is Mr Greengrass the right person to ask for? Or would we need to speak to someone in their orders department?"

"Try Charlie first off – mention my name and I'm sure he will point you in the right direction."

The conversation moved on to more relaxed topics until it was generally agreed that the evening had been very pleasant but that everyone was busy one way or another and needed to go to bed before it got too late.

When Alex and Mel got back to the pub, they found several messages had been left for them – two telephone calls from Jimmy Manley, one from Melpomene's Mama, and a note from Pat Georgiadis.

"I'm afraid that these will have to wait until the morning," said Alex, "I need to go to bed right now!"

"I won't argue," said Mel, "but I can't help wondering why Jimmy phoned twice – let me see, once at 7.30 and again at ten o'clock. What is it now – eleven o'clock? I'll try him at home."

Chapter 32

Detective-Inspector Jimmy Manley answered the telephone rather grumpily, but as soon as he recognized Melpomene's voice said, "Excuse my tone of voice, but I had just dropped off. I suppose you were out somewhere when I tried before, the operator just said you were unavailable. I've got something to tell you that you might like!"

"Is it about the maroon Lagonda, Jimmy? We actually spotted it ourselves in a village near here – we were going to tell you the registration number, but maybe Cec Thomson got there first!"

"No, actually he found four Lagondas starting with VO7, but we haven't been able to narrow it down, except that they were all sold by the same dealer in Nottingham. Quite often dealers get a batch of plates ahead of sale, to save trouble when they make the deals. So what was the number of the one you spotted, Mel?"

"It was VO 7721, Jimmy, was that one of the ones you found?"

"Yes, it was, and we already looked up the owners of all four, and – let me see – that one is registered to Lady Hyacinth Killane, of Hazel House, Willis Avenue, Harpenden!"

"Very interesting, Jimmy!" said Mel, "Apparently she is not averse to lending her car to ruffians, most likely without enquiring about their purpose! I had a look in the pub at Sandridge, outside which it was parked, and the only candidates in there at the time were a couple of heavies in suits. I managed to lip-read a couple of fragments of their conversation before I slipped out because they were beginning to take notice, and one said something like, *'His lordship will want to know more than that!'* I concluded that he was talking about Ellsworth, and that they were on some errand on his behalf."

"Let's leave it at that, for now, Mel – I really need my beauty sleep – and we'll take up the chase from this end in the morning. And I suppose you and Alex have plans too – give my regards to him and say good night!"

"I will, Jimmy, and some time we'll let you know all that we've found out – quite a rich treasure-trove, in fact!"

When Melpomene finally hung up, she realized Alex was already asleep, so she shrugged, bathed and joined him. He didn't even stir when she kissed his forehead!

The next morning they were both full of energy, ate a hearty breakfast, and went back to their room to read the papers and plan the day's activities. Mel had related her conversation with Jimmy to Alex over breakfast, and had already started to put together a list of things to do, which she related to Alex once he had thrown aside the papers, saying, "The country seems to be going to the dogs regardless of our efforts, Mel!"

"Jimmy will tell us more about the Lagonda, once he and his colleagues have found out, but meanwhile I want to talk to Irene some more, to ask her whether she managed to smuggle everything back into Killane's filing cabinets safely, and I want to tell her what we've found out about the ownership of the Lagonda. Are you going to make follow-up enquiries with Mr Greengrass, that business colleague of Graham Fletcher? And there's Madeleine Stone, the PR officer, too – we should think what, if anything, we are going to approach her with. Can you think of anyone else, Alex?"

"We must think carefully whether we're going to try and eavesdrop at the dinner that the Ellsworths are putting on for Lord and Lady Furlong. I thought I might drop into the Blue Boar before we go back to London and see what the arrangements are in the dining room. I had a vague thought that we might be able to get ourselves seated where you could do some lip-reading. What do you think, Mel?"

"I know I've done this trick a couple of times to good effect, Alex – but it depends on a clear view and only works on speakers who articulate clearly – I learnt it at a school for people with impaired hearing, where everybody was wanting to make themselves understood. At a dinner party, the eating tends to get in the way! I think we should think along other lines, my dear. How do you feel about hiding under the table?"

"Hiding might be the way to go – but not under the table. There might be some more comfortable places with good audibility for conversations – I'll check all that out if I can when I visit the place. The other thing, Mel, is that I've been looking at this rough telephone directory that Gwyneth gave us – it could be very useful, and she has also added a list of the members of Senate, with their contact details when they're from outside the university. Have a look through it – she said she'd scribbled on it, but I shall have to ask her what the various annotations mean when I telephone her next. It's nearly nine o'clock, so she should be at her post by now – let's see."

But when Alex rang the university switch, it was not Gwyneth who answered but another woman, who said in rather flustered tones, "Who would you like to speak to, please?"

"Well I actually wanted to speak to Gwyneth Fletcher – is she not there?"

"I'm afraid she hasn't turned up for work yet, and I haven't had a chance to make enquiries, as I'm getting a flood of calls and I'm a bit slow at it!"

Alex told Mel what was happening, and said, "I'll telephone her home – she could be sick or something!"

Clarissa Fletcher was rather concerned, saying that Gwyneth had left on her bicycle at the usual time and had been perfectly fine, "Perhaps she's had a puncture or something – would you be able to check? We have only one car and Graham has already left for work in it!"

"Tell me what route she takes, Clarissa, and we'll drive from the university towards your house and see whether we can find her – don't worry, it's probably something minor, like a puncture or the chain coming off!"

He made some notes of the route and rang off. Mel said, "Should we check with the police whether there have been any road accidents, Alex?"

"No, that would be a bit premature – let's hop in the car and check her route out! You drive and I'll navigate and keep my eyes open."

They started at the campus and began following Gwyneth's route in reverse, towards Harpenden. There was very little traffic – they supposed that those who drove to work had already got there. Gwyneth had chosen to avoid the main north highway, using by-roads instead, but they were able to retrace her ride with the help of Clarissa's directions.

Just as they were approaching the district where the Fletchers lived, Mel exclaimed, "What's happening ahead – there's a car in the ditch and an ambulance! Oh dear, this doesn't look good!"

Chapter 33

Melpomene drove past the car and ambulance and drew up at the side of the road. They walked back and Mel asked the ambulance driver what was going on.

"Not very much, actually, madam, the driver won't need to go to hospital – he was shaken up, but not injured. He's sitting in our ambulance and getting his breath back. We'll send for a breakdown vehicle as soon as we've made a phone call. We were called out by a young woman passing on her bicycle, who saw him skid on some loose gravel and leave the road. She telephoned from that house over there – that's where my mate has gone now – and then waited by the car until we arrived, told us her name and address in case the police wanted any witnesses, and then set off again."

"Was she a Miss Gwyneth Fletcher?"

"That's right, madam, do you know her? As I said, she got back on her bike and carried on – she said she was late for work."

Mel thanked him and then said, "Alex, since we're nearly at the Fletcher's house, why don't we go and put Clarissa's mind at rest?"

This they did, and Clarissa immediately telephoned the university to find that Gwyneth had arrived safely and was taking calls!

She said, "Thank you both ever so much for bothering about Gwyneth – I should think you're ready for a cup of coffee and a biscuit or something by now, am I right?"

"That would be very nice, Clarissa!" said Melpomene, "Could we impose on you a little and make a couple of telephone calls, please? We were about to do that when we found out about Gwyneth."

"Please go ahead, it's the least I can do!"

So Alex rang the university again, and when Gwyneth answered, said, "We were so relieved to find that you're safe – did you actually see that motorist leave the road – was he speeding or what? But what I really want to talk to you about is the draft telephone list you gave us. You've added a lot of annotations – do they have specific meanings, Gwyneth?"

"Yes they do, Alex. Mostly I've put a 'T' a 'D' or a 'B'. I tried to keep them obscure in case the list ever falls into the hands of the opposition! 'T' means I trust the person, 'D' means I'm dubious, and 'B' indicates a bad person, for example, Sir Desmond Killane – you'll see that there is a 'B' by his name and a 'T' by his p.a. – Irene of course. And there are many names that are not annotated because I have no information or have never spoken to them. Can you follow all that?"

"Thanks, Gwyneth, we'll have a serious look through the list soon. And when we need to telephone anyone at the university, we can take note of your annotations. Now, perhaps you could connect us with the palatial student edifice where resides Pat Georgiadis, please. I see it's listed as 'Hall of Residence No. 1' – but there doesn't seem to be a Number 2."

"You're right, Alex – that's just this university getting ahead of itself again – here we go."

Pat was soon called to the telephone, and Alex said, "We got the note you left at the pub, Pat, what's this 'interesting development' of which you speak?"

"Yes, Alex, I didn't want to be too explicit in a note that could be read by anyone, and in fact I would rather not discuss it over the telephone – can you come here later this morning? I'm seeing my supervisor in a few minutes, but I should be finished with him quite quickly – how about eleven o'clock? – I can offer you coffee!"

"See you then, Pat!"

Melpomene said, "I'd better ring my Mama back before we do anything else – she probably simply wants to be assured that I haven't been involved in any gun-fights or been kidnapped, poor darling!"

She was right, so she gave Lady Cynthia a brief account of their latest exploits, emphasizing that, so far, they had not confronted any gangsters, though they had had some suspicions! She rang off, assuring her mother that she would keep her informed of anything serious, then said to Alex, "While I'm about it, I'll check in with Marjorie and Winnie, though they would have got in touch if necessary."

The secretaries reported that not a lot had happened there, but that they were not wasting the time, but had gone together to an office-equipment supply house.

Winnie said, "It's up to you two, of course, you are the bosses, but Marjorie and I really fancy getting one of these new Dictaphones, so that we can record a conversation or telephone call and transcribe it without having to use shorthand. Do you want us to get details and prices?"

"Yes, go ahead by all means," said Mel, "we don't promise anything, but make a good case and we'll take it seriously. No mail, I assume?"

"Nothing special, Mel, and no telephone calls of any interest. When do you think you'll be back?"

"We'll probably drive down this evening, so we'll see you both in the morning!"

"Right!," said Alex, "Let's go and see what Pat wants to talk to us about."

They found that Pat hadn't got back yet, but Penny welcomed them, offered them tea and biscuits, and asked what they had been up to lately. Mel told her about the scare they had just had with Gwyneth and said how pleasant it had been to meet Olive's family.

Then in came Pat, clutching a pile of papers, and saying, "Frank Tennyson is pleased with my progress and has promised to make enquiries about funding for a trip to Greece, so that's very encouraging. But I should tell you something I just found out that could be very significant for our enquiries – or your enquiries I should say, but I'm feeling quite involved!"

"We're all for that, Pat!" said Melpomene, "We would not get very far if we kept ourselves at arms length from all our friends and collaborators – so please let us have it!"

"Well it started, like a lot of things round here, in the public bar of the Poacher – while you were away at the Fletchers' I suppose. Penny and Anthea and I were having a quiet chat over a drink or two when a couple of large men in suits breezed in, talking excitedly. They collected a pint each and sat down at the next table, still going on, and we had no difficulty overhearing them. I wasn't paying much attention at first, until the red-headed one said, 'So, Arthur, we'll 'ave ter get up early if we're to make it to 'Arwich in time for the boat! If we're late, we'll never 'ear the last of it from 'is nibs!' and the other replied, 'For a Lord 'e can be very, very nasty!' and they both laughed, but, I thought, a bit nervously."

Chapter 34

"Right!" said Alex, "We'd better telephone Jimmy straight away – if someone can intercept the boat we stand a chance of nabbing these blighters in the act – whatever that act might be! Excuse me, ladies!"

He left the room and went down the hall to the shared telephone and in a few minutes was back.

"Jimmy, like me, believes this pair are the ones who have been spotted driving the Lagonda before. He'll make contact with the customs and excise people at Harwich port who he spoke to recently and he's also going to talk to the police there. He'll ring back here and report progress. That pair said they would have to leave early, so I hope we'll be in time!"

"Oh, sorry!" said Pat, "I should have acted more urgently! But you and Melpomene were out of reach until you telephoned me this morning, and I didn't think it through properly I'm afraid!"

"Never mind, Pat – no use crying over spilt milk!", said Mel, "What we need to do now is plan our next moves. I've been wondering about ways of getting more information out of dear Sir Desmond, to add to the useful stuff that Irene brought us. He should be tied up with the Senate meeting again today, so maybe we could rifle his office more thoroughly, with Irene keeping watch – if she's willing. Once we've had word from Jimmy I might give her a call – she'll be able to tell us whether we need to keep a watch out for other people in the administration, like Mr Benson, the admissions officer, who is in the same building and knows Alex by sight."

"That was when Alex was pretending to enquire about postgraduate law courses, wasn't it?" said Penny, "If I may ask a naïve question of you, Melpomene, have you done any more about pursuing the enquiries about enrolling that you told us about when we met at the tennis court that day? You said you were interested in sociology or psychology masters to add to your qualifications in Social Anthropology."

"You are dead right, Penny! I should pick up that line straight away!" said Melpomene, "One of your other tennis friends, Jo I think, mentioned an academic who seemed to be more interested in a candidate's chest than in her academic record – can you recall what department that was?"

"No, sorry I can't, Mel. But it suggests a possible scenario – if you were willing to do a bit of acting!"

"Oh, Mel enjoys that!" said Alex, "I've seen her in various roles, ranging from estate agents to a gas inspector and an elderly flower-seller! I'm sure she could doll herself up to appear to be someone who is relying more on her glamour than her other qualifications – what do you say, Mel?"

"I'm not much in the chest department, my dear, but I think I can bat an effective set of eye-lashes! I'll work on this!"

Just then, they heard the telephone ringing, having left the door open to hear it better, so Alex went to pick it up.

After a few minutes he was back.

"Some good news, some not so good!", he announced, "to start with the latter, we missed the boat, so to speak. There were only two due to dock at Harwich this morning, one from Hook of Holland, which we all think was the one we're after. This had already discharged its passengers by the time our message reached Customs and Excise, and they had nothing to report. There were the usual couple of amateur smugglers, they said, with more than their legal allowance of spirits and tobacco, but nobody serious. The other ship was a freighter from Esbjerg, Denmark, and it is still in the process of tying up. These freighters sometimes take a few passengers, so when they come ashore, they will be scrutinized too. And Jimmy has left a message for our Danish colleague, Jens-Olle Pedersen, just in case he knows anything."

"But you said there was also some good news, Alex, what was that?" asked Melpomene.

"Well, the police were looking in different ways from Customs, and managed to spot Lady Hyacinth Killane's Lagonda, number VO 7721, parked in a Harwich side-street near the Quay Hotel! No signs of any occupants, but they've got a plain-clothes officer keeping the car under surveillance. And if I know Jimmy, he'll have arranged to have someone check out the guests at the hotel, particularly those patronizing the bars. And since our blokes set off early this morning, they may be looking for lunch before they drive back. Of course, Jimmy will let us know about developments!"

"Are we to telephone him again, or will he ring here?" said Mel, "I would like to make some calls myself, but I'm hesitant to tie up this telephone for fear of missing him. Tell me, Penny or Pat, is there another one that I could use, or should I go back to the Poacher?"

"Come with me, Melpomene," said Pat, "there's actually a coin-operated telephone in the refec – make sure you've got plenty of pennies and shillings if you need to call long distance!"

Melpomene duly collected change from everyone present and Pat walked with her to the refectory and pointed out a small room in the corner of the entrance hall. "I was expecting a red kiosk!" said Mel, but Pat said, "The university refused to have one – I suppose Lord Ellsworth thought it would bring too plebeian an air to the place! Anyway this one works fine, and there's even a seat!"

The first number that Mel rang was Crabbe and Crabbe. Marjorie answered and was brought up to date with recent activities.

"Any interesting mail or telephone calls?" Mel asked.

"Well yes, as a matter of fact!" said Marjorie, "There's a thick bundle from Philip Seaward, with a covering letter explaining that it summarizes all the illicit transactions perpetrated by Henry Jackson and Elspeth McCracken at Finchley Hospital. He has also been asked to keep some days free next month so he can give evidence at their trial for embezzlement. I expect you and Alex will be needed, too, but there hasn't been a summons yet for that one, but you will be called for other counts those two are up for – particularly the ones about issuing threats against your Mama, Mel!"

"So, what about telephone calls, Marjorie?"

"Yes, one from your Mama – not just her usual check-up that you and Alex are safe, but an appeal for you to note in your diary that you are expected at Woodhampton Castle for Christmas – it's only a couple of weeks away, remember! And, finally, there was a call for Alex from his friend Archie Staples – he said to tell you that he'd found out some very interesting stuff about Daniel Flint KC, but that he would rather talk to you face-to-face once you are both back in the office."

"Well done, Marjorie! As I told you, we will probably drive back this evening. See you in the morning, with any luck!"

Chapter 35

The next call on Mel's list was to Irene, "We've assumed that Killane will still be tied up at the Senate this afternoon, Irene, is that right?"

"Yes, Melpomene, and after the business is over they will all adjourn to Lord Ellsworth's mansion for a ceremonial dinner, which means that Sir Desmond won't be back here at all today. He has given me strict instructions that I should take care of any business that turns up and not bother him except in a major emergency!"

"Excellent, Irene! We've had the mad idea that we might take the opportunity to rifle his office while you keep cave! What do you say to that, is it taking things too far?"

"No problem, Mel! I've already convinced myself that he is an out-and-out crook, so that would be entirely justifiable as far as I'm concerned. You should try to avoid the Senate lunch break, however, because there's a slim chance he might slip back to his office at that time if he's forgotten anything. Half past two or later should be safe. I just skimmed off the obvious stuff previously, so I shall enjoy seeing how real detectives approach this task! Do you know where to come? We're on the top floor of the main building, Room 30, it's well labelled."

"Are there any danger spots nearby, Irene, like offices occupied by people we're not sure about? I'd hate to have someone pop out and confront us, even though we usually have a cover story prepared in these cases. If you don't foresee any such difficulty, we'll probably have something to eat in the refec and then come and find you at 2.30."

Since Jimmy Manley had not telephoned by the time that Mel had rejoined the others, she telephoned Mile End Road station but was told he was still away from his desk.

"So, when he wants to get in touch with us," she told the PC who answered the telephone, "ask him simply to call the main switchboard at Harpenden University, and we'll leave word with Gwyneth, the operator, where we can be found."

That done, they all went off for lunch and the usual pleasant conversations with the girls, who were eager to hear all the latest developments.

Just after 2.15, Alex and Melpomene tapped on the door of Room 30, which bore a plaque reading 'Sir Desmond Killane, Bt., Deputy Vice-Chancellor and President of the Academic Board.'

They heard Irene call, "Come in!" and she welcomed them to her office, which served as an ante-room to Killane's sanctum.

"Most of the files are kept here in this room, of course, since I am the one who attends to correspondence and filing, but he has the one cabinet of which I spoke, which he believes to be private, not knowing that the same keys fit them all. I concentrated on those files when I was selecting them to show you, but since our session at the pub I've been rummaging around out here. I've only been here a few weeks, so I haven't had much chance to find out just what he has accumulated here. But what I have discovered is that a lot of the drawers and files have names which don't seem to make a great deal of sense!"

"Interesting!" said Melpomene, "Are you saying that your predecessor as his personal assistant has made mistakes, or what?"

"No, I think these file names are deliberately obscure, like a sort of private code. I'll show you what I mean – let me see – yes, here's a good example! The file has a label saying 'Ginger and Cinnamon', while the documents inside appear to be inter-office memoranda on standard university forms, covering a range of topics. I'll read out the title lines of the top few – 'complaint about impolite behaviour', 'failure to record conversation', 'excuse for overlooked deduction' and so it goes on. There are details in the bodies of the memoranda which go on to explain further, and each one ends with a hand-written comment, such as 'dealt with' or 'bring up on Friday', most being initialled 'DJK'. His middle name, I have found, is 'Jerome' – but I've never heard him use it except for with these initials."

Mel said, "Let me pursue these a little further, Irene. Do they refer to particular people? Can I see, please? – Oh, just initials again, but the same ones seem to come up repeatedly. I think we'll have to put these aside for the moment – perhaps patterns will start to emerge as we go on."

Alex was beginning to fidget, "We ought to avoid getting fascinated with these puzzles, Mel, we're not solving crosswords, after all! Tell us, Irene, have you come across anything more sinister? Instructions for murders or kidnaps, perhaps? No. sorry, I'm getting silly now! We suspect that Killane is dishonest and we're finding that he is devious too, but maybe he's been careless once in a while. What I would suggest is that Mel and I settle down with a heap of files each, and quickly but carefully work through them looking for any interesting features. If we take a drawer at a time, we can make sure that we replace the files in their original order so that we don't leave any evidence of our work. And we can ask Irene for explanations sometimes. Can you give us some typing paper for us to make our notes please, Irene?"

Alex and Mel were occupied for the next couple of hours, making comprehensive notes and replacing the files in the drawers as they went, while Irene undertook to search through Killane's diaries and take note of what seemed interesting, asking Alex or Mel when she couldn't tell what might be important or not. Then, in his desk drawer, she found a little black notebook with initials and telephone numbers. She showed Alex, and he said, "We can't risk taking it of course – can you copy out as many of the entries as you can for us?"

Irene also made it her duty to keep everyone supplied with cups of tea and two sorts of biscuit.

At half past four, Alex looked at his watch and said, "That will have to be enough for today – we need to go back to the pub, pack up and head back to London. Shall we eat en route, Mel, or should we telephone Mrs M to get something ready for us?"

"Eat on the way I reckon – we've left it a bit late for Mrs Mountain – she would do her best, as she always does, but it's unfair on her. Before we go, Alex, we ought to try Jimmy once again. I think Gwyneth goes off watch at about this time, didn't she tell us?"

This time, they caught Jimmy at the station. He said, "I've got a long story to tell you, but I might leave it and come round to your office in the morning and relate it at length, rather than giving you a rushed version now – but I will tell you that our efforts at Harwich really paid off, I'm happy to say! Drive carefully now!"

"Wonderful, Jimmy – we'll see you in the morning and Archie Staples in his turn will share with you the low-down on Daniel Flint KC."

Chapter 36

"Before we set off for London," said Alex, "I'd like to check out the dining room at the Blue Boar, and it might not be a bad idea at the same time to reserve ourselves a table for next Wednesday, using an alias, of course. If Lord Ellsworth's party is of substantial size, it might take up a good part of the room's capacity that night, and it would be annoying to miss out."

It turned out that the Blue Boar was a large, mock-tudor building in the centre of Harpenden High Street. In the foyer, Alex approached an attendant and asked who he should speak to about a dinner booking. He and Mel were taken to a counter, where the attendant rang a small bell and the maître-de appeared.

"We'd like to reserve a table for next Wednesday evening, if possible, to celebrate our wedding anniversary. Can you do that?"

"Let me see in my book, sir and madam – I know we have a private function on that evening, but we should have at least one of our balcony tables free, I'm sure – yes we have indeed."

"I'm not sure what you mean by a balcony table", said Melpomene, "I don't think we would like to be tucked away in a corner somehow!"

"Let me show you, madam, please come with me," and they were led to a staircase which gave onto a view of the dining-room, which held at least twenty tables of various sizes, with only a few occupied at that early hour by parties of two or four diners.

"As you see, we have two tables in this balcony, and a further two over on the far side. The main room can, of course, be arranged in a variety of ways, depending on the function, whether a municipal banquet or a wedding reception. I don't believe you will feel segregated at all."

"Very well then," said Alex, "let us make a booking – I presume it would be a good idea to choose a menu now?"

Once they were well on the road home, Alex said, "I don't know whether you noticed, Mel, but I was able to follow the conversation of the diners we saw down below us then. There might be much more of a buzz on the night of the dinner, but I still believe that between the two of us we may be able to pick up anything that's going – whether they talk about things that are of interest to us is another matter – we can but hope."

"And apart from what we can overhear," said Melpomene, "we might be able to get a sense of the relationships between the various participants as well, by observing their nonverbal communication. I'll explain this more later, Alex, but first let's look for somewhere to eat – I'm feeling a little peckish now, but it was rather too early to dine when we were at the Blue Boar."

"There's a turning to St. Albans coming up, Mel, how about trying there?"

There was a good selection of eating places on the main street of the town, so they agreed to try an Indian restaurant that looked promising. Over their lamb rogan josh, Melpomene drew Alex' attention to a well-dressed couple seated a couple of tables away, too far to overhear what they were saying.

"He's smiling a lot, you see, but isn't looking directly at her, while she is pretending to eat, but is just pushing things about on her plate while she fidgets in her seat. I reckon that we're observing a relationship in the final stages of collapse here. Maybe we'll see later how this comes out. Meanwhile, I'm going to attend to my meal – it's rather delicious, don't you think!"

As Melpomene and Alex were finishing their meal with Indian sweetmeats and coffee, the couple they had been observing earlier paid their bill and left. The man tried to guide his friend by taking her arm, but she shook him off and turned and glared at him, before collecting her wrap and striding out of the restaurant without a second glance at her companion.

Mel said, "Was I right or what?" and Alex replied, "Very impressive, my dear!"

When they arrived back at the flat, Mel spent a few minutes telling Caroline of some of their exploits and then said, "But now, I'm about ready for bath and bed! If you could make us some hot chocolate, that would be a kindly act – we'll tell you more at breakfast time, but we're anxious to get to the office good and early as Jimmy Manley and Archie Staples have promised to give us comprehensive reports of what they've found out so far."

"Good, Melpomene, so I won't bother you with a minor domestic matter until the morning!" said Caroline.

"Oh, you can't leave me dangling like that, you know! At least give me a clue or I'll be inventing all sorts of stories and possibly dreaming about them!"

"Well, it's hardly high drama, Mel! Mrs Mountain's daughter is about to present her with her first grandchild – so for some strange reason Mrs M wants to take a few days off! She's gone to her daughter's place already to await the District Nurse and the midwife, but no doubt she'll telephone and tell you all about it tomorrow. They don't have the telephone on at the daughter's, so we can't ring her there. She lives in Greenwich, I think."

At breakfast the next day, they hadn't had any such call, so Caroline undertook to pass on any messages as soon as she heard, and Mel and Alex set off for the agency.

Winnie and Marjorie were happy to see them and were eager to hear everything, but had a couple of things to report first.

"Detective-Inspector Manley rang and said he'd be here about ten o'clock, but we haven't heard from Mr Staples yet – yesterday he just said he would come here this morning some time," said Winnie, "but Marjorie took a call a few minutes ago, I don't know who that was from."

Marjorie answered, "It was someone called Irene Bradshaw, Mel. She sounded a bit anxious. She had just missed you at home – could you ring her as soon as possible, please – at her home, not at the university – I'll get her for you, shall I?"

"Hello, Irene!" said Mel when she answered, "What's afoot – nothing dangerous, I hope!"

"No, not dangerous, but fairly serious, Melpomene! After you left yesterday, I fussed around, mainly to make sure that we had left no evidence that the place had been done over! I even wiped the filing cabinets that you and Alex had opened. I didn't bother with my own prints, of course. And, just as I was getting ready to lock up and go home, Sir Desmond arrived.

"I said I was surprised, as I thought he was going to go straight to the dinner, and he replied 'As did I, Miss Bradshaw – but that was until Lord Ellsworth started abusing me! So I stormed out!' As you might think, I was dumbfounded!"

Chapter 37

"So did he elaborate?" asked Melpomene, "Or was he still too much in a kerfuffle about it?"

"Actually he seemed to have calmed down – perhaps during the walk back to his office – and went on to say that he had decided to go to the dinner anyway and try to smooth things over, but he added, 'I still don't really understand – Ellsworth seemed to be accusing me of disloyalty – perhaps someone has been deliberately spreading malicious gossip! At least I can rely on you, Miss Bradshaw.' It will be very interesting to see how all this plays out, Mel – have you any recommendations on what I should do? I feel rather guilty about working against him while he seems to trust me."

"I see what you mean, Irene – but just keep on reminding yourself that these are men who have committed murder, or at the very least connived at it! But try to play it very cool when you see him again this morning. I'll speak to you again later – we have a couple of key visitors coming to the office very soon, and I'll certainly keep you informed of whatever develops."

Mel and Alex brought the secretaries up to date with what had been happening at Harpenden, and they gave the notes they had made in Killane's office to Marjorie so she could type them up tidily.

"Anything you can't follow, just ask – we can still remember most of what we had in mind, I expect, but we don't want it to fade."

Then Jimmy Manley and Cec Thomson arrived, so they had to be plied with tea and jam tarts while they too were told a little of what had been happening in Hertfordshire.

"First, we're impatient to hear about your adventures in Harwich," said Melpomene, "Did you catch the red-headed thug and his mate?"

"We certainly did!" said Jimmy, "My blokes from Mile End Road got assistance from the Harwich people, so they could keep an eye on the Lagonda as well as visiting the public bar of the Quay Hotel, which they reckoned would be the most likely place for them to fetch up. There was nobody matching the description we gave them in the bar when they arrived, so a PC and a sergeant, both in civvies, just settled down with beers in the corner and waited. And then the four coves we were expecting swaggered in – the red-head and his mate in their suits and the pair from the tube station – the tall bald guy with the big red nose and the moustache together with his bank manager friend. We'd instructed our men to keep observation, not to engage with them unless it became necessary – they had been issued with side-arms as a precaution, of course."

"Could your people pick up any of their conversation, Jimmy?" asked Alex.

"They certainly could! There was a certain amount of banter, like *'did you have a nice holiday with them Dutch girls'* and a smooth crossing and so on, then the red-headed heavy explained to baldy and his mate that they had been brought back to England for a further job, *'His Lordship reckons the heat'll be off by now, but in any case you'll be kept well out of sight – Lord E. has a country house near Saffron Walden where you can stay indoors and play cards or whatever until you're needed again, which'll be in about a week – you'll be told all about it in good time.'* Our sergeant made sure to keep notes and got ready to follow them when they left, expecting that they'd head for the car, which was a good guess. What these crims often forget is that if they use a distinctive car it'll be easier for us to track – we had a police car already waiting up the lane where the Lagonda was parked, and we'd circulated its description and number to all the cars in the district in case we lost it."

"So, were your people able to follow the car?" asked Alex.

"They certainly were! To cut a long story short, the minders drove the tube villains to a pricy-looking Saffron Walden mansion, where we now have some watchers ensconced in a barn just outside the estate, with good views of the house and its exit ways so that they can keep an eye on them. A sergeant from the Harwich station arranged this for my people with a friendly farmer – there is no love lost between Ellsworth's people and the neighbours, for a number of reasons, it turns out! And, just in case, some of our men from Mile End Road followed the red-head and his mate in the Lagonda all the way back to Harpenden, where it was garaged at the Killanes' place."

"So I suppose," said Melpomene, "that all we can do now is wait and watch – unless, I suppose, we can pick up any information somehow. Sooner or later, instructions about the next task for these murderers will have to be given them, but what I'm wondering about is how long you will have to wait before nabbing these two – after all, it's pretty clear that they are the ones who murdered Cyril Speedie at the tube station."

"I agree with you, Mel," said Jimmy, "we certainly have a good case against them, which will probably be substantiated by our eye-witnesses, but as long as we don't let them slip away we stand to gain more by keeping them under observation. If they do manage to escape, I can tell you there'll be hell to pay – I could be stripped back to a uniformed PC! But my blokes who are watching them are well aware of this and they are very competent, so I'm only a wee bit worried!"

"You said that the neighbours at Saffron Walden were not happy – what's that all about?" asked Alex.

"It seems that there are several sides to this – the farmer whose barn we are camped out in was saying that the new people were behaving 'just like townies' – leaving gates open, letting their guests' children trample the growing crops, and even frightening the animals – those sorts of ignorant behaviour. Mr Bassett has been up to the big house to complain on more than one occasion and was treated very rudely. He thinks it's not the owner's family who are living there, but some of their business friends – they all have big cars that they drive through the lanes at high speed! You'd think that if they're using the place as a retreat for their murderous accomplices they would try to keep their heads down, but if anything they are only drawing more attention to themselves!"

"My word, Jimmy!" said Melpomene, "You must be quite satisfied with that days' work! What do you plan to do next? We've been trying to gather some dirt on Killane, with the invaluable help of Irene Bradshaw, and it's becoming more and more clear that he and Lord Ellsworth are into skullduggery up to their aristocratic necks! So when do you think that some sort of direct confrontation would be the way to go?"

"We'll need to lay more groundwork first, Mel. We have a tremendous advantage here – we know that Ellsworth and Killane are at the centre of things, and we know exactly where they are at the moment, so we can take our time building up an even stronger case. There must be other scoundrels lurking behind the scenes, and I'd like to flush them out, but carefully!"

Chapter 38

Marjorie said, "While you were talking, Winnie and I have been typing up most of the notes you made about Sir Desmond's files – do you want to show them to Jimmy while he's here? We've made a first shot at putting them under various headings, and any people's names that were mentioned we've underlined in red. We made carbons, so we've got two sets."

"Oh what a joy it is to have the services of clever secretaries!" said Alex, "Let's see, Jimmy, we found that some of these were filed under peculiar names – it looks as though Killane had his own system of codes, or maybe they are just random, intended to put snoopers off, so we're ignoring them for the moment."

"Thanks, Alex," said Jimmy, "can you spare a copy of these notes for a while? I'll ask my WPC, Jennifer Sweet, to look through them, since she has had nothing to do with this case so far. A fresh eye can sometimes see patterns that have escaped people familiar with the subject-matter. I'll have to go back to the station now, but Cec can stay for a while, so you could pass him anything else you think might be helpful to us."

After Jimmy left, Alex asked DC Cec Thomson what he'd been up to lately. "Nothing terribly exciting," said he, "but now I've been put on your case, I am looking forward to some real action – it would have been nice to be on the Harwich excursion, but I was tied up at the time with a series of shop-liftings – I managed to collar a sweet little old lady who was running a very professional service for clients looking for cheap jewelry and watches. She would ask to see a range of items and somehow one or two would fall off the counter into her shopping bag. But it takes more than a whiff of 4711, a shy smile and a twinkle of the eyes to fool yours truly!"

They were all enjoying yet another round of tea and jam tarts when Archie Staples arrived. While he was enjoying a cup, Melpomene told him all about the activities of the day before including the larceny of Sir Desmond's office.

"You will be particularly interested in what I've found out about Desmond's lady wife, then," said Archie, "I was looking up Daniel Flint, KC in 'Who's Who' and found that he has two siblings – an older brother called Martin and a sister called Hyacinth Elizabeth. I looked them both up, of course – Martin is some sort of business man of no particular interest to us, but I found that Hyacinth, as you may already have guessed, since that name is not common, is married to Sir Desmond Killane, Bart!"

"So – wheels within wheels!" said Mel, "I wonder whether the late lamented Cyril Speedie had any inkling about this connection? I gather, Archie, that you have been tracking down more of Flint's activities – anything else to do with Harpenden?"

"Not directly, Mel, but as well as the cases that Mr Speedie had told you about before, there were several that I thought had rather a dubious flavour about them, even though they had proceeded through the court system without any difficult questions being brought up by either the opposition or the judge. Of course, I was inclined to be suspicious of Flint's behaviour and was deliberately looking for trouble."

"And found some, no doubt, Archie! I recall that the previous occasions we heard about often provoked criticism from judges – is he still making himself unpopular with the judiciary?"

"Not so much, Mel, he seems to be taking a more subtle approach now – for instance he has started praising his opposing counsel instead of denigrating him or her, but in such terms as to leave a nasty smear behind – let me read from a recent transcript – this is Flint: *'My Lord, I must commend Mr Sandwich for his thoroughness, but would point out that not all the evidence provided by his witness has been verified by reliable third parties, such as the police. It is right that a young counsel should be enthusiastic, but he will discover over time that this should be tempered by caution and by meticulous checking. I refer in particular to the witness' statements as to time and location ...'* And he goes on in this vein, sowing doubts in the minds of the bench and jury about the quality of the evidence. If this case were a single example, it could be passed over, but Flint's approach is becoming entrenched. I have brought you notes of over two dozen cases that make my point, Mel and Alex. Please study them at your leisure."

Alex said, "That's very valuable, Archie, but I was hoping that you might uncover some actual misdemeanours as well as that rather technical stuff. And it would really be good if you had found out that he is associated with criminal gangs, like the notorious Ellsworth-Kinnane mob!"

"I've been keeping the plums for last, Alex and Mel! As I told you before, Daniel Flint works out of the same chambers as I do, and I have made it my business to become friendly with the chambers clerk, Ron Bisley. He and Flint have had a falling-out, and Ron was only too eager to pass some very interesting information to me. I have collated it all and made explanatory notes, and here it is, as well as the transcripts of some of the cases that Flint has conducted. You will find that it makes fascinating reading! And there are some names mentioned that might be familiar to you."

"Cyril Speedie thought that Flint might in the pay of some criminal organization – did you find any evidence of this sort of thing?"

"Not in the case notes themselves, Alex, but I also got Ron Bisley to show me the carbons of various letters that Flint had got the chambers staff to type up for him. Being a well-run office, copies had been kept as a matter of routine – and Flint was not interested enough in the day-to-day work of chambers to know this – he had his own file copies and that was that. I didn't get to see any inward correspondence or replies to his letters – he wasn't that naïve! But there were references to these replies in follow-up letters that he sent out. Have a look at these, for example: *'Thanks for doing that, Desmond, I'll certainly get in touch with your Mr Hammond if I need any pressure applied to the opposing client!'* And here's another: *'Lady H is happy to make her limousine available to me for getting BD to the North when necessary, I'll let you know how it goes.'* No prizes for guessing the identity of Lady H! There are some other names mentioned that don't ring any bells with me, but maybe you or your police contacts will be able to fill in the gaps.*"

Melpomene said, "We'll spend many happy moments going through all this stuff, Archie – are these our copies to keep, or do you need them back?"

"They're all yours, Mel, I got Betty to type up copies for you. She gets very enthusiastic about your investigative activities – if you can think of other ways of involving her, I'm sure she'd jump at the chance!"

"Well, at the very least, you two must come over for dinner some evening – it's our turn – but it would be nice to see some definite outcomes to all this first! Now, let's go through some of this stuff together, and it might start making a lot more sense!"

Chapter 39

Over the next few hours, with a break for lunch when Archie was introduced to Guiseppe's trattoria, a number of lists were drawn up, one of questionable names that Flint had mentioned which needed to be followed up, and another of cases in which it seemed to Archie and Alex that legal niceties had been bypassed.

"If Betty still wants to be involved," said Alex, "she could rely on her position as a solicitor to visit the Law Society Library in Chancery Lane to follow up these cases. I suppose, Archie, that she's familiar with its facilities?"

"I think so, Alex, but as well as tracing these cases, she could also enquire whether Flint has ever been reported to the Bar Council for improper behaviour. He has certainly trodden close to the edge from time to time, but it will be interesting to find out whether judges have ever pursued this further."

When Archie had left, Melpomene said, "Now to catch up on some telephoning. I have some people in mind that we need to call, but have there been other callers lately, Winnie and Marjorie?"

"Only Irene Bradshaw," replied Winnie, "but you've already spoken to her this morning. What about your postgraduate friends at Harpenden – do you need to keep up with them?"

"You're right, Winnie! I'll telephone Pat Georgiadis and see whether she has anything fresh to give us. And there are also some calls we must make tonight or tomorrow, after the senate meeting has finished. We actually met an external member of the senate at the pub who might be a useful source of information – being an outsider he's very unlikely to be enmeshed in the webs of intrigue at the university. His name is Colonel Randolph Stavely-Roper – I think Alex has his card, but anyway there can't be many Stavely-Ropers in the telephone book. We were meant to see him and his wife at the Poacher this evening, but what with one thing and another we won't. We'll have to apologise about that when we telephone!"

Marjorie nudged Winnie, "When Irene rang, it was after Mel had talked to her this morning – she probably had something else to say, so we should try her again. Shall I get her, Mel?"

When Irene answered she said, "A few things, Melpomene – they could possibly wait but I'll tell you anyway. The first is that Sir Desmond came back at the end of the meeting in a nasty mood again. He wouldn't tell me precisely why, but he muttered that he had about enough of being treated by Ellsworth as some sort of lackey. He threw some papers on his desk and went off in a huff, so, in my new role as a spy I had a look at them. There was a copy of the agenda, with his scribbled comments, but what interested me was the report of the Economy Drive Panel. This was quite thick – about thirty pages of typescript – so it would take me a fair while to copy it all. Would you like me to summarise it for you, Mel? Killane has scribbled on this, too, so maybe the sections he has paid attention to would be the most valuable for us – there I go again – I should say valuable for you!"

"Never mind about that, Irene – you are showing yourself to be a vital part of our team! Was there anything else?"

"Yes, there was an envelope addressed to Sir Desmond and Lady Hyacinth Killane. It had already been opened, so I had no hesitation in looking at the contents – there was a nicely engraved invitation from Lord and Lady Ellsworth to attend a dinner at the Blue Boar next Wednesday – 7.00 for 7.30, evening dress. But, more interesting, there was a seating plan! I have already made a copy, because I thought it might come in handy for you and Alex. The original is safely back in the envelope now! Shall I post it to you at your office – do we have enough time?"

"Oh yes please, Irene – this is going to be extremely valuable! As well as showing who is sitting where, it is a list of people who Lord and Lady Ellsworth hold in good regard – with the possible exception of Desmond Killane! It will be extremely interesting to compare this list with the ones we are building from Daniel Flint's cases and his correspondence."

"Oh, that reminds me – I was quite surprised, Mel, to see that Daniel Flint and his wife Rosemary are invited to the Ellsworths' dinner!"

"You mightn't have been so surprised, Irene, had you known that he is Hyacinth Killane's brother! It looks as though family connections are playing a part in these intrigues – almost as they are said to do in the Sicilian Mafia! We look forward to receiving that seating guide and any notes you have prepared already. We'll keep in touch – we might drive up early on the day of the dinner and talk to you some more, if that's all right. How would you feel about us coming to your house? We could park a little distance away if you prefer."

"Yes, that would be fine, have you got something to write down my address – it's not too near the Blue Boar. See you on Wednesday – I'll telephone you if there's anything else."

Alex had been listening on the extension, so there was no need for Mel to relate it all to him.

"I've had an idea," he said, "I intended to telephone Randolph Stavely-Roper anyway, to ask him what happened at the senate meeting, and now I'll also enquire whether he's prepared to let me have a look at his copy of the report of the Economy Drive Panel, if he hasn't an immediate use for it. Can you get him for me, Winnie, here is his card – it has his home number as well as his office."

It was Felicity who answered the telephone, so Alex made his apologies at having to miss their bridge appointment – Felicity told him not to worry since there would be more opportunities. Then Randolph came to the telephone.

"How did the senate meeting go, Randolph – any shocks?"

"Oh, if only there had been – I'm used to boring business meetings, of course, in my line of work, but that one takes the biscuit. I didn't realise what a lot of petty backbiters academics and university administrators can be! And when it came to the famous Economy Drive, the claws were out too! There are at least two opposing factions at work here, and the Deputy Vice-Chancellor made no attempt to conceal that he was on the side of those who want to save money at all costs, down to the elimination of whole departments! If I were an academic in any of the Arts or Humanities areas, I would be reading the want ads in the Times every morning."

"Yes, we have heard anecdotes about this sort of thing, Randolph, and that brings me to a request I would like to make of you, if you think it proper. Would you be willing to lend us your copy of the Panel's report? If you have annotated it at all this would be especially valuable too. Of course, we would not disclose the source of any information we might use in pursuing our investigations, that goes without saying!"

"I have no problem with that, Alex – I'll send it right away!"

Chapter 40

"Now I'll finally get round to telephoning Pat!" said Melpomene, and when she had been found and brought to the telephone, gave her a summary of what had been found out with Irene's help.

"And I've got something for you, Mel – this might knock your socks off! Do you remember a girl called Pam who was one of the tennis players when we first met? She and her friend Jo are trying to get into the M Econ programme. Anyway, I bumped into her in a bookshop in Harpenden yesterday and asked her how it was all going. To my surprise she blushed and got all confused and stammered, 'I might have to go elsewhere instead!' Being a pushy little person, I took her elbow and persuaded her to come and have a cup of coffee and then asked her what this was all about!"

"I think I might have done the same," said Mel, "was it another case of pressure being put on her?"

"It certainly was, and of a completely unexpected kind. As part of the qualifying process, candidates were interviewed by pairs of academics from the Economics school. Pam said that nothing untoward happened during her interview and in fact she felt that it had gone quite well and she had a good chance of being accepted, but as she left the room, one of the academics, a woman in her mid-forties, Pam thought, came out too, fell into step beside her and said that she was a pretty girl and must have a lot of boyfriends. Pam was a little shocked and said, 'Not really!', whereupon the woman took her arm, squeezed it, and asked her if she would like to come back to her office for a sherry! At that point, Pam made some excuse and escaped."

"Had it been me, I might have gone along with the woman in sheer curiosity – but then, I'm the adventurous type!" said Melpomene, "I suppose this was what decided Pam to find another University!"

"Not immediately, Mel – she felt she had invested a lot of time and effort in her application – so she thought she would make enquiries about this Dr Shawcross before she came to a decision."

"Who would you ask in such a case?" Mel wondered.

"She went straight to the Dean of Economics," said Pat, "he just nodded a bit, made notes and said he would look into it. Pam tried to explain that she had nothing against anyone's sexual preferences but that she thought that the woman's behaviour was rather predatory, especially since she was in a position of power. Pam was still waiting for a response from the Dean, so she decided she had better look for help elsewhere! She felt rather reluctant about this, but she plucked up her courage and made up her mind to talk to the secretary of the Students' Union, a woman she's known for some years."

"I asked what she said, but Pam told me she hadn't been to see her yet, but was hoping to do so the next day, so then I asked her whether she would like me to go along with her – she agreed with some relief! That's going to happen this afternoon after the Union Council meeting – I'll let you know the outcome, Mel."

"Any other news for us, Pat? Any more intruders into your digs?"

"Not really, Melpomene, but there has been a prowler spotted a couple of times. When he or she was seen the first time it was quite late in the evening – after that we all got together and agreed to keep a special eye out, even to the extent of going for little strolls round the area – in twos and threes – before going to bed every night."

"You said 'he or she', Pat – does that mean that nobody got a good look? And have there been any attempts to follow or confront this person? Maybe he or she is just a harmless tramp or an innocent person going for evening strolls. Anyway, if there are further sightings, let us know and we'll work out what we can do about it, such as following him or her surreptitiously. Let me know what happens with Pam, please. We shall be in Harpenden on Wednesday – we're going to attempt to eavesdrop on a dinner the Ellsworths are throwing at the Blue Boar for a certain Lord and Lady Furlong and some mysterious friends, apparently from Lisbon."

"That's interesting, Melpomene, I wonder if that's the same Monica Furlong who I crossed swords with at a labour conference last year? She wasn't listed as a Lady then, just as a researcher from a provincial university, Bristol or Birmingham, as I recall. We got into an argument during one of the symposia, on the topic of participant observation – she is a supporter of the 'hands-off' school and I was making the case for getting involved in the local politics of social movements. All very wishy-washy stuff, but she got quite intense!"

"Oh, Pat – that is an area I could easily get interested in myself! But I have to remember I'm strictly an applied social anthropologist, not a theorist! I wonder what the connection might be between the Lisbon contingent and happenings at Harpenden? This is all getting very interesting! We'll hear from you later!"

On their way back to the flat in the Riley, Mel brought Alex up to date with what Pat Georgiadis had told her. He said that this made their visit to the Blue Boar even more interesting, and complained that it was a pity that there was no way of recording the conversations apart from taking shorthand notes.

"I thought about Dictaphones, but they are clumsy and need to be plugged into the mains – and anyway you have to speak directly into a microphone, so it wouldn't pick up general conversation. And I read about a device called a wire recorder that's being developed in America, but they probably cost more than a house! So I'd better just take plenty of sharpened pencils and a shorthand pad."

"I'm more concerned about not being sprung!" said Melpomene, "If they spot us listening intently and taking notes, they'll probably think we're a couple of reporters from a society magazine or one of the tabloid newspapers! I'm sure Lord Ellsworth would not welcome that! We either need to be very inconspicuous or adopt the role of vapid society time-wasters – this is meant to be our wedding anniversary celebration, so perhaps we could exploit that idea somehow, what do you think, Alex?"

"Well, Mel, perhaps you could become rather tipsy and I could assume a disapproving posture and remonstrate with you, while taking notes as a diversion!"

"Ha, ha, Alex! Surely the last thing we want is to draw attention to ourselves. How about we write our notes on a pad and pass it back and forth between us as though we are exchanging messages of love? Alternatively, let's not make elaborate plans which might turn out to be inappropriate and instead just play the whole thing by ear!"

"You're right, of course, Melpomene – as usual!"

Chapter 41

The next day, they hurried to the office straight after breakfast to wait for the postman. While they waited, Mel explained to Winnie and Marjorie why they were so keen.

"We're expecting two important documents this morning, the seating plan for the dinner tomorrow as well as the report of the Economy Drive panel, which is of interest in a couple of ways – not only to identify the departments or individuals that are being targeted for cuts, but also because I hope that Colonel Stavely-Roper has made notes about those members of the senate who expressed opinions one way or another. We'd like one of you to go through these notes and see if any familiar names pop up. How about that, Winnie – are you comfortable with that? Good! It would really be useful to get our hands on the minutes of the senate meeting, but I suppose that would be treated as a highly confidential document."

She went on, "But in a way I'm more interested in the seating plan. This will of course tell us who has been invited to the dinner so we will know who is speaking when we're there – and I'm hoping that those mysterious Portuguese contacts will be listed – and it should also give us a feeling for a hierarchy of the guests – the key people who are seated on the top table, or at least close to His Lordship, and the minions who have been relegated to the minor places. This will help me to add to the chart I've been working on."

Then the telephone rang. Marjorie answered it and said, "Hello Caroline – oh that's wonderful – mother and baby both well I hope? Here's Melpomene – Mrs M is now a grannie, Mel!"

There followed a longish conversation, and then Mel passed on the details to the others, "Girl, easy delivery, seven pounds, blonde hair what there is of it, going to be called Louise Christabel – the latter after her grandma, so now we know Mrs M's first name, which we never did before! We'll have to think of a nice christening present, but no hurry! We could send a card now, though, Caroline will know the address."

Then there was a ring at the doorbell, and the postman handed over a pile of letters and a thick package. Marjorie checked through them and handed Mel the package, which turned out to contain the Economy

Drive panel report, and also a letter from Irene with the seating plan for the dinner, as well as some less-interesting mail, such as bills.

She handed the first back to Marjorie, saying, "Please go through this and make a list if you can of those members of the senate who are noted as being for or against the proposed cuts. Some people, I suppose, possibly including Randoph Stavely-Roper, won't have commented one way or the other. I imagine there would be a full list of the members of the panel – this will be interesting, too! But I'm more interested at the moment to see what the seating plan will tell us. Alex – let's look at this together, shall we? I see, there are two large tables set out – that establishes a de facto order of importance right away!"

As they had predicted, the principal guests, Lord and Lady Furlong, were seated each side of the Ellsworths in the centre of the main table, and facing them across that table were two people with names that could be Portuguese – Senhor João Castelo Branco, and Coronel Gustavo Oliveira.

Alex seized upon these names, "Let's telephone Adrian Fitz-Hugh and see whether the international police organization has them on its books – Ellsworth referred to them as 'wealthy friends from the continent' but also reminded Killane that they had met before, so I have my suspicions! Can you see if you can get Sir Adrian please, Marjorie?"

"And I'll ring Gwyneth a bit later," said Melpomene, "and get her to put some titles to some of the other guests, if they work at the university. We know that Gerald Benson is the admissions officer, and that Malcolm McArthur is the Vice-Chancellor, and I think that Henry Hanson is the Bursar, but there are many others I can't place. Of course some guests might come from outside the university, so Gwyneth might not know them. I'll ring her once we've tried Adrian – I don't want to tie up both lines."

Marjorie reached Sir Adrian, and when Alex spoke he was very glad to hear from him, saying that things had been rather formal and boring recently, though quite busy. He took down the two Portuguese names and said he would get his contact in Lisbon onto them straight away and ring back when and if he had anything to report. Alex thanked him and gave him a quick background to the case, to which Adrian replied that he had read about the murder in the tube station, but of course had had no reason to make the connection with Crabbe and Crabbe.

When Mel rang Gwyneth, she said, "I thought I had put people's departments on that draft telephone list? But I'll happily update any entries for you – just tell me the names."

There were in fact several amendments, and as Mel had thought, Gwyneth didn't recognize some of the names, thinking they were probably not university staff. But there was one such that she nevertheless had some information about.

"I've had a number of inward calls from this gentleman, Mr Armstrong, over the past few weeks. Normally he simply states his name, wanting to speak with Killane, but on one occasion he got his secretary to make the call, and she said, 'William Armstrong, of Wolverhampton Office Supplies here, calling Sir Desmond Killane, could you put him through, please?' So I did so, and waited a little to make sure that Mr Armstrong picked up. He has a pronounced accent, like someone from Birmingham, and his grammar is atrocious, judging from the snatches I've heard!"

"Thanks for that, Gwyneth! This Armstrong must be quite important to the university, since he's been seated, with his wife, on the top table – very intriguing!"

Alex, who had been listening said, "If he has frequent telephone conversations with Killane, he might have had correspondence, too. Can you get me Irene Bradshaw, please, Marjorie, and I'll see whether that name rings any bells with her."

But before she could make the call, the telephone rang and it was Adrian Fitz-Hugh asking for Alex.

"We drew a blank on Senhor Castelo Branco, I'm afraid, but our Lisbon office has a file on his friend Coronel Oliveira, and a very interesting file at that! As you might surmise from his title, he is a former army officer and was for a time the Military Attaché in the Portuguese Embassy in London, until he became *persona non grata* and was forced to resign! I'm still investigating him through my contacts in the Foreign Office in an attempt to find out how he blotted his copybook!"

"É mesmo?" said Alex, "Which means 'oh really?' – This was a favourite expression of a Brazilian friend I had at University College, whose eyebrows were always shooting up whenever he heard something surprising! I think he went back home, or I might recruit him as a translator! But, if our Coronel worked in the embassy, he must be fluent in English, anyway!"

Chapter 42

Alex hung up on the call to Adrian and announced that now he could ask Irene about William Armstrong, so got Marjorie to ring her.

"Ah, Irene," he said, "we've spotted a Mr Armstrong who has been given a prominent place on the seating plan, and we wondered whether you could find any interesting correspondence between Killane and him. Gwyneth tells us that they have frequent telephone conversations, so they apparently do a fair amount of business. Of course, it is entirely possible that Armstrong is a legitimate businessman – apparently he runs an office supply company."

"Well, Alex, I'm afraid I can't do anything about it at the moment," said Irene, "because Killane is working on papers in his office – can it wait until this evening? I could have a look once he's gone home if you need the information before the dinner tomorrow."

"We are only guessing anyway, Irene, so don't take any risks! Meanwhile, our high-level police contact has found that one of the Portuguese guests has some sort of dubious history, so we're awaiting details. Melpomene and I will certainly be busy little bees tomorrow evening – we mustn't forget to eat!"

As there seemed to be no business remaining that wouldn't wait until the morrow, Alex and Melpomene went home to a dinner cooked by Caroline.

"I'm not quite up to Mrs M's – Christabel's – standard," she said, "but my main problem is that it takes me twice as long to do anything as she does! I hope you enjoy it anyway – it's one of her mainstays, Osso Bucco, followed by bread-and-butter pudding!"

They certainly had nothing to complain about!

Over breakfast the next day, Melpomene and Alex discussed what they would do before going to the Harpenden dinner.

"We suggested to Irene that we might call into her home to see what else she had to tell us," said Mel, "and we can find out whether she has been able to dig up anything about this William Armstrong. If we get there around six o'clock that should allow for her spending a little while at work after Killane has left – he'll need to get himself togged up in his soup-and-fish before going to the Blue Boar, so I bet he'll leave work a bit earlier than usual."

"That reminds me," said Alex, "I've been meaning to check what you'll be wearing for the dinner – I assume it will be something posh, as we are, ostensibly celebrating our anniversary – I shall wear my DJ, of course."

"I thought I might wear that slinky number in green that I bought for the St Luke's embassy banquet. But given that English hotels are not always well heated, I'll also take my black satin quilted evening jacket with the monkey-fur trim. It has the additional advantage of a pocket suitable for a small pistol! You never know when you might need one in a hurry – we're venturing into enemy territory, after all, and the dress is so slinky I couldn't pack a nail-file without it showing!"

"Point well taken, Mel! I've become accustomed to thinking of a shoulder holster as a normal accessory to a dinner jacket!"

"Let's go to the office for a while, Alex, to see if there have been any interesting telephone calls or letters. I'd like to call Jimmy Manley and put him in the picture, too."

The post hadn't come when they arrived at the agency, and Marjorie and Winnie hadn't taken any telephone calls yet, so Mel took the opportunity to call Detective-Inspector Manley.

"I don't know whether you've been keeping track, Jimmy, but this evening we're off to the Blue Boar at Harpenden for Lord Ellsworth's grand dinner – not as guests, I should point out, but as observers and eavesdroppers. Has Adrian Fitz-Hugh talked to you recently? He's on the track of some Portuguese people who have been especially invited to that dinner, and it turns out that one of them has been bending his diplomatic privilege to the extent that he was declared *persona non grata* and had to leave the Portuguese embassy. Any developments with the tube-station desperados? When we last spoke, you had the house where they are holed up under surveillance."

"Nice to hear from you, Mel – I have nothing more to report on our watch over the Saffron Walden house, but you will be interested to know that Jennifer Sweet was as thorough as usual and has made a couple of fascinating discoveries when going through the notes that Irene Bradshaw made on the files from Killane's office and also from the dinner seating plan. Maybe you didn't know, but your indispensible secretaries have been passing me anything they thought might be relevant."

"I'm very pleased they have, Jimmy – by now I'm confident that Marjorie and Winnie would never disclose anything that we wouldn't want you to know!"

"Such as what, Melpomene? Only kidding! Anyway, Jennifer found that at least three of the people she checked have something they would prefer to hide! For a start, Henry Hanson the Bursar, has a record! Admittedly it goes back a long way – he was prosecuted when he was an undergraduate at Manchester University for misappropriating funds from the student Rugby Club. He was sent down for that, but talked his way into another college and got qualified as an accountant. How he got his present job beats me, Mel – Harpenden couldn't have done much checking at all! The others that WPC Sweet found were not as blatant – Benson, Alex's contact from Admissions, has outstanding fines for motoring offences, speeding, defective lights, that sort of thing, and a woman in the records department, Sybil Hartley, was held in police cells overnight on two or three occasions for 'disreputable behaviour in a public place, to whit, the saloon bar of the Lion and Thistle public house, while under the influence of alcohol or drugs' – apparently she has a tendency to remove her clothing for any excuse! Jennifer was considerably amused as she read the court transcripts – I heard her laughing from the next office!"

"Congratulate Jenny for me, please, Jimmy! She's done some good work there!" said Mel, "We're going home to change after lunch, and then we shall drive to Harpenden to see what else Irene Bradshaw has for us before we turn up at the Blue Boar. We hope we shall not be noticed by the diners, but we're prepared for trouble should it arise. Of course we'll let you know what transpires – see you later!"

"I hope you won't think that I'm being over-cautious," said Jimmy, "but I'm putting some precautions in place myself. I won't disclose any of them to you now, it'll be best if you forget this and don't start looking round and trying to pick out my men – do you recall your visit to the opera that time? I'll say no more, except to wish you good hunting!"

"Thanks a lot, Jimmy, we'll all keep our fingers crossed anyway – Alex sends his regards, too!"

Chapter 43

After lunch, and before they went to change, Melpomene said, "I may be cautious, Alex, but I think I'll ring Irene before we go, just to confirm when we'll be getting to her place. Oh, hello, Gwyneth – how is everything going with you? We're just about to set off for Harpenden, so I thought I would check in with Irene Bradshaw first. Could you get her for me, please?"

"Actually, Mel, she doesn't appear to be in her office at the moment – I just tried to put in a call for Killane and he answered himself, in a peeved voice, and explained to the caller that his p.a. was not there, so he would deal with the enquiry himself if he could. I hung up then and let them get on with it. I tried Irene's home telephone, but there was no answer there either – I do hope she's all right!"

"So do we!" said Mel, "I think we have her home number, but tell it me again, in case. We'll try again while we're en route – you first, in case she's got back to her office, and failing that at her home – this is a bit worrying, given the whole background!"

Half-way to Harpenden, they pulled into a pub and asked if they could use the telephone. Once again Gwyneth said she hadn't returned to her office, but that Killane was not in, either, so Alex thanked her and said they would try her home number. This time, a woman answered, saying she was Mrs Bradshaw, Irene's Mum. "Oh no, she's not here, Mr Crabbe, I just got in with the shopping – she must still be at work, since her car's not here!"

"Thanks very much, Mrs Bradshaw, I'll check at the university. Would you happen to know the registration number of your daughter's car? I might try to find out whether it's on campus."

"I do, as a matter of fact, it's an easy one to remember because it's like her initials – IB 1920. Do you think she might be in trouble – I'm beginning to worry now!"

"Don't get too concerned, please – there's probably a very simple explanation, like a car breakdown or something."

"Oh, she's in the AA, so in that case she might have rung them up or flagged down one of their patrols. Will you let me know when you find out anything, please?"

They thanked the pub landlord and paid for the calls, then set off again.

After a few miles, Melpomene spotted an AA telephone box and said, "Alex, why don't we enquire whether there's been a distress call from Irene?"

The woman who answered the AA telephone said, "Let me see – where might it have been? I see, somewhere in Hertfordshire or thereabouts. No, I've just checked, and I'm afraid we've got no record of a telephone call from a member called Bradshaw, however, our motorcycle patrols aren't always able to report in straight away if they've been attending a problem. Could you call back in an hour, say? We might know more by then."

Mel started to get worried, "I think we should ring the police as soon as we get a chance, Alex, either at a police box, or when we get to Irene's house."

When they got there, her mother had still not heard, so Melpomene tried the AA again, still with no luck, so she telephoned Jimmy, who was still at the Mile End Road police station. She related the story, while Alex took Mrs Bradshaw to the kitchen to make tea, and said, "It's a white Morris Cowley saloon, registration number IB 1920. What I'm worried about, Jimmy, is that her investigating activities might have been rumbled by Killane. We know that he and his gangster mates are capable of extreme measures to keep people quiet."

"Thanks for letting us know so promptly, Mel. I'll get on to the Hertfordshire constabulary and get them to put out a general call. Unless the car has been hidden or dumped, it should turn up soon – a semi-rural area like that is easier to comb than it would be in London. I shall soon be on my way to Harpenden with a couple of my blokes, but, as I said before, I shall avoid contacting you in obvious ways. If we spot you or Alex and have some news, we'll signal you somehow."

Alex and Mel sat for a while with Mrs Bradshaw over tea and cakes, and then made their excuses to leave, Mel saying, "We've booked a room at the Blue Boar, as we didn't want to drive back to London tonight, and it gives us a chance to freshen up before we go to dinner. I gave our police friends your telephone number, so if they hear anything you will be informed. If Irene gets in touch with you, as she probably will, you could try the Blue Boar for us, up to about seven fifteen. We are booked under the name Musgrave, my maiden name."

In the lobby of the Blue Boar they checked in and asked if there had been any messages. The receptionist checked the pigeon holes and shook his head, "We always put a note in your box about any telephone calls, but there's nothing. The boy will take your valise and show you to your room – it's on the same floor as the balcony where your table is reserved for this evening – Jamie will point out how you get to it. If you require refreshments in your room, just ring the bell. Do enjoy your stay and your dinner, Mr and Mrs Musgrave."

At about 7.15, Mel and Alex strolled along to their balcony table. As they sat down, a waiter asked if they would like an aperitif, but they thanked him and declined. He left and Mel and Alex went to the rail over which they found there was a good view of the activities below, without having to show themselves too much. There were waiters standing ready, and a few of the guests, some carrying champagne glasses, were looking for their places and chattering together. Alex spotted Benson and his partner, but recognized no-one else – the principals and their main guests had not yet entered.

Then, as they watched, a couple who must be Lord and Lady Ellsworth came in, escorting another couple with whom they were conversing, presumably the Furlongs. Behind them were another pair, who they assumed were Desmond Killane and his wife Hyacinth. As each of them took their seats, Alex referred to the seating plan and confirmed their identities, as well as many of those who followed, ticking them off as soon as he was sure.

Then their own waiter came back in, saying, "We are offering you the same menu as we are providing for the banquet, so the selections are a little more limited than is usual for us. However, we can offer you a choice of soups to start – Chef was asked to make sure that the whole menu was typical of the district, so there are brown Windsor and a game consommé to choose from to begin with."

They both opted for the game consommé, as Mrs M was famous for her brown Windsor, and they took a sweet white wine to accompany it.

Mel said, "We shall at least have a good meal tonight, even if we learn very little about the opposition – but it is early yet! By the looks, the noble guests have gone for the brown Windsor, while the Portuguese contingent are trying the consommé!"

Chapter 44

Any hopes that Melpomene and Alex may have had of overhearing the diners' general conversations were soon dashed – the overall buzz was too much. Alex pointed out, however, "There will be speeches, no doubt, so we have a good chance of picking up interesting items from them. Meanwhile, we can simply observe whether or not there are interactions between key people. For instance, Lady Hyacinth has hardly exchanged a word with anyone since she sat down, not even with her husband."

Melpomene added, "This may partly be because Killane has been in animated conversation with his other neighbour, Coronel Gustavo Oliveira, with both of them waving their arms about. Look – the Coronel has just banged his fist on the table, laughing uproariously! Perhaps Killane just told him a joke."

"The second Portuguese gentleman, on the other hand," said Alex, "is sitting rather glumly, hardly exchanging a word with his neighbour who is – let me see – none other than Mr William Armstrong – perhaps Senhor Castelo Branco is bored by talk about office supplies, or maybe his English is not up to deciphering Armstrong's thick Birmingham accent."

The waiter came to collect the soup plates and asked them whether they would take Chess River rainbow trout or local white-clawed crayfish. Alex chose the trout, but the more adventurous Mel went for the crayfish. When the waiter brought their selections, he also handed Alex an envelope, saying that it had been given to him on the stairs by a man he didn't recognise. When he had left, Alex opened it and read it out, "All it says is 'IB safe. JM.' – good old Jimmy! What a relief! – no doubt we'll get the full story later!"

The meal proceeded well, and Mel and Alex had no difficulty enjoying their choices of the various main courses, all with their local attributions, until desserts and cheeses were brought, and Lord Ellsworth rose to his feet and tapped his wineglass as a signal.

"Lord and Lady Furlong and other distinguished guests. I think we can all agree that the proprietors of the Blue Boar have presented us with a fine selection of the Hertfordshire cuisine, accompanied by French and Portuguese wines – I'm afraid that there is no tradition of local wines here or anywhere else in England unless you count elderberry wine – which I don't!"

There was discreet laughter and clapping, and Lord Ellsworth continued, "Some of you will be aware that there have recently been proposals for changes to Harpenden University, an establishment which is close to my heart, as many will know. Without going into the trying details, I will simply mention that there have been funding difficulties, and that a special panel was convened to make recommendations to address these. Over the next few days, the Vice-Chancellor, the Deputy Vice-Chancellor and the Bursar will circulate to all staff – and to those students who might be interested – a series of documents laying down these recommendations, which will be acted upon by the Senate after due consideration. This evening is not an appropriate occasion for me to detail these, but I will take this opportunity to make one announcement which is germane. As many of you may be aware, the campus and buildings of this university reside on an area of my ancestral estate which I happily made over for the purpose a few years ago. Due to changed circumstances, the lease over these facilities has been sold to a consortium of eminent businessmen in this country and on the European continent, particularly in Lisbon, under the chairmanship of Lord Furlong, here. The legal transfer of these assets will be accomplished in stages, but will be finalised by the end of the current financial year, in April next."

There was an excited buzz among the guests at this, and Lord Ellsworth held up his hand and continued, "I can assure everyone present that the rights and conditions of every member of staff will be given full and humane consideration over the transitional period. If, as cannot be avoided, there will need to be some redundancies, there will be adequate notice given, of no less than three months, and often longer."

There was an even more intense buzz, and many guests got up and moved around to talk to others, Lord Ellsworth rapped his glass for attention once more and said, "Coffee and liqueurs will be served at the table, but you are all at liberty to take them into the adjacent lounge – through those double doors, ladies and gentlemen – where you may relax and talk to others. There will be other hotel guests there, you may mingle freely, of course."

Melpomene and Alex looked at one another with eyes wide. "Should we mingle, too?" said Mel, "Or would that be pushing our luck too much?"

"For myself, I'd like to spend a while contemplating that shock announcement," answered Alex, "there is obviously going to be a lot happening now, and I can't guess at the implications yet – I think there will be plenty more investigative work for us to do now. But, as far as I can recall, you have never yet confronted any of the guests we have seen here tonight, while I have had words with at least one, Benson, the admissions officer."

"Right, then – I will go and mingle and see if I can pick up anything – you stay here for a while, Alex, so I'll know where to find you if necessary. Pass me my wrap – I'd feel happier being armed, and my Beretta is in the pocket, loaded and cocked."

When Melpomene reached the lounge she found that a substantial proportion of the dinner guests were already there, as far as she could judge. She didn't attempt to engage anyone in conversation, preferring just to wander about and try to pick up scraps of what others were talking about. Then she spotted Sir Desmond Killane, whom she and Alex had identified from the seating plan earlier. He was talking at last to his wife, Lady Hyacinth, so Mel wormed her way through the crush towards them, just as he said, "Excuse me, my darling, I need to go!" and made his way toward a door marked 'Gentlemen'. As he went, Coronel Oliveira fell in behind him, and they both disappeared.

Mel turned her attention to Lady Hyacinth, who had started to talk to another woman, both waving their hands about and making excited remarks, like "What a surprise!" and "Fancy bringing this all out at dinner!"

And then there was the sound of a shot from the gentlemen's convenience and everybody fell silent. The other Portuguese man, Senhor João Castelo Branco, drew a revolver from a shoulder holster and plunged through the door. After a moment, he re-emerged, shouting "Policia! Policia! Assassinato! Assassinato!"

Immediately, a man in a suit, who had run toward the door at the sound of the shot, displayed a police warrant card to the crowd, drew a pistol and went into the toilets with Branco. Mel, to her great surprise, recognised Cecil Thomson!

Chapter 45

Someone grasped Melpomene's arm, and she spun round, finding to her relief that it was Alex. He drew her aside – most of the others were craning to see what was going on, while a small group of men came into the lounge, one announcing, "Police here – please make way. Nobody is to leave the hotel until we say so – we will take witness statements as soon as we can."

"When we heard the shot," said Alex, "I could see that most of the people still in the dining-room reacted immediately in amazement, as you might expect, with the notable exception of Lord Ellsworth, who I was watching particularly. I think he must have been expecting something of the sort, because he merely directed a slight nod at Lord Furlong. He then started exclaiming and moving toward the doors of the lounge, but by then he was a bit late to appear natural to me. Look, Mel, he and his noble companions are in a group over there near the doors, chatting together and smiling, as though this were a perfectly normal evening's entertainment. Ah – here comes Jimmy and some ambulance men with a stretcher!"

This latest group disappeared into the toilets and soon the stretcher was wheeled out, bearing a body, apparently a corpse since it was completely covered, and taking it from the room. Then Cec Thomson emerged, leading Sir Desmond Killane in handcuffs, looking rather battered and staggering a little, with blood coming from under bandages on his forehead. There was no sign yet of DI Manley or Senhor Branco. As Cec spotted Melpomene and Alex standing there, he said, "The detective inspector has cleared you two to go in, as long as Mel doesn't mind seeing the inside of a Gents!"

So, to curious glances and mutterings from the crowd, the two pushed open the door and went in, to find Jimmy facing Branco, also in handcuffs, but sobbing uncontrollably.

"I've cuffed this gentleman as a precaution – he admits pistol-whipping the injured man, but has protested that he found him standing over the body of his colleague and was compelled to act. His English is not good, and I have no Portuguese, but he was able to convey that much through words and gestures. He will be interrogated in full, of course, as soon as we can locate an interpreter. I called you in, Mel and Alex, because you can probably tell me who all these people are!"

Alex explained, "I can tell you their names, and I know a fair bit about the one who did the shooting – you've heard us speak about him often before, he is Sir Desmond Killane, and it looks as though he has just added another murder to the list of his crimes. The dead man is another Portuguese, Coronel Gustavo Oliveira, but apart from the fact that he and his friend were invited to this dinner by Lord Ellsworth for some reason, we know little about him, except that our friend Sir Adrian Fitz-Hugh told us he was dismissed from a position at the Portuguese embassy – we haven't yet found out much more. The friend's name is Senhor João Castelo Branco – I have mixed feelings about his restrained behaviour in merely pistol-whipping Killane instead of shooting him!"

While this was going on, the guests were all asked for their names and addresses and mostly allowed to leave. In fact, some of them headed straight for one of the bars, presumably to steady their nerves with a drink or two and marvel over their experiences.

As they left the toilet, Melpomene and Alex told Jimmy that they would join these people, saying, "We might pick up some interesting remarks – everyone's guard will probably be down by now!"

"Yes, you're probably right!" said Jimmy, "And I've instructed my men to take note of whether people leave in a hurry or what. I suppose most will have arrived here by car or taxi, so we'll note that as well. I hope nobody who has over-indulged will attempt to drive themselves, or we'll need to run them in! I hope we've got enough cars available. By the way, we're taking Killane and Branco, as well as Lady Hyacinth, who wanted to accompany her husband, to the local Harpenden nick for questioning, which will probably be done tomorrow morning now. I don't know whether the CID branch here has good interrogators, but we'll find out."

Mel and Alex went to the saloon bar, just as the landlord was announcing that since there had been a private function, and given the exciting events, the police had agreed to relax the normal licencing hours and so the Blue Boar would stay open until two in the morning if necessary.

At this, there were cheers from a small group of men, who Mel assumed were opportunistic locals.

The only people in the bar that Mel and Alex recognised from the dinner were the bursar and his wife and various minor characters – Lord and Lady Ellsworth and their main guests, the Furlongs, had already been whisked away in a limousine. Nevertheless, they still circulated discreetly to see what they could pick up – in the event, nothing much, except that Henry Hanson, the bursar, appeared to be having some difficulty reassuring his wife that she had nothing to fear.

"That of itself is rather significant!" murmured Mel, "We must delve further into that gentleman's activities later."

After an hour, Mel and Alex decided to go to their room, had their baths – in this establishment, there were private bathrooms with showers attached to the bedrooms – made hot chocolate using the facilities also provided, and went to bed to sleep the sleep of the just.

The next morning after a very satisfying breakfast, they settled their bill and asked where they could find the police station, which turned out to be within walking distance, so after putting their luggage in the Riley, they set off for the station.

The desk sergeant understood immediately who they were and said, "Detective-Inspector Manley, and our CID people are talking in the CID office. They said to show you in when you arrived, Sir and Madam, it's this way."

Jimmy introduced them to the uniformed inspector in charge of the station, Inspector McManus, and said, "We've located a Portuguese speaker to interpret for us – we simply rang up the Romance languages department at the university, but the telephone operator, your friend Gwyneth, put us straight on to a Dr da Silva, who she knew was a visiting lecturer from Oporto. Very bright lady, your friend! He told us he would be able to get here within the hour, after he's finished his tutorial. We assured him there was no great hurry."

"Last night," said Inspector McManus, "we had to take Sir Desmond Killane under guard to the local hospital to get him patched up. It turns out that he has no broken bones, just a gash and contusions. The gun he was hit with was an army-issue Colt revolver, quite a heavy weapon, so he was lucky – in a sense!"

Chapter 46

"What about Lady Hyacinth Killane?" asked Melpomene, "Are you holding her in custody?"

"No, we have no grounds as yet," answered McManus, "so we have put her in the WPCs' rest-room with a cup of coffee – she said she didn't want to go home until she knew what was happening with her husband. He hasn't been formally charged as yet, pending us getting more information from Senhor Branco when he is questioned by Dr da Silva, who, by the way, should be here shortly. I have told the desk sergeant to bring him straight to this room when he arrives. And we haven't really questioned Lady Hyacinth – we might do that when we have more to go on."

"Will Alex and I be permitted to sit in on the interrogation of Killane and Branco, Inspector?"

"I would prefer not, as it is not standard procedure," was the reply, "but I will put you in the next-door interrogation room and you will be able to hear most of what is said through the thin walls. We'll have a short-hand writer, PC Jerrold, there and he will prepare a full account. However, Mrs Crabbe, if you would like to sit with Lady H and have coffee with her, I would not object if you were to question her in a chatty way!"

"Good thinking, Inspector McManus! By now she will be somewhat anxious about everything and might let her guard down to an apparently sympathetic woman. She doesn't know me, so I must give some reason for being there – I don't want to disclose that I'm a detective. Maybe I'll introduce myself as the Hon. Henrietta Musgrave! And I could say that I was there while the police are deciding whether or not to charge me with driving under the influence!"

"I have no problem with that as long as you haven't told me about it!" said McManus, "Come along to the WPCs' rest-room and you can chat with her. You can't really be seen to be taking notes, so you'll just have to remember what she tells you if she comes out with anything significant!"

Melpomene found Lady Hyacinth sipping what was obviously not her first cup of coffee, and chain-smoking highly-scented Turkish cigarettes. She offered her cigarette case to Mel, who declined, saying that her mouth already tasted like the bottom of a bird-cage, "I'm ashamed to admit that I had a few glasses too many of French vermouth after all that excitement at the Blue Boar last night! I'm being held while they decide whether or not to charge me with drink-driving – I keep telling them that I just sat in the driving seat to have a rest! I think they might be inclined to believe me – I told them that I was an honourable and that my Mama is a Lady! I'm Henrietta Musgrave by the way, can I ask your name, and what they're holding you for? – If they are, that is."

"My name is Hyacinth Killane, and I'm married to Sir Desmond of that ilk – for the moment that is! He's going to be charged with murder, probably – he was the one that did the shooting last night – and I'm hoping that this will be sufficient grounds for divorce, so I can escape his clutches! Oh, my dear, I am going on a bit – it must be all this coffee! Please forgive me for burdening you with my problems!"

"Please don't apologize, Lady Hyacinth – feel free to get everything off your chest – I'm happy to listen to you if it helps! You must feel very strongly about your husband to talk like that about escaping him – do you want to tell me more? Does he beat you, or what?"

"Oh, no – nothing as simple as that, Henrietta, if I may use your first name. The situation between us has been building up over several years, since I discovered to my shame that he is an out-and-out embezzler and worse! Recently, he has forced me not only to keep his secret but actually to help him in his nefarious pursuits, for example by allowing his horrid underlings to use my car for some of their criminal activities. When I protested he threatened me with social disgrace and worse – I have even started fearing for my life, and last night's events have confirmed to me that he would actually go to such desperate lengths. So now you can see why I am fervently hoping and praying that he will now be safely locked away!"

At that moment a PC appeared at the door and beckoned to Melpomene. "Oh dear!" she said, "Maybe they're going to charge me now! I hope to see you later, Lady Hyacinth – don't despair!"

Outside, she was taken to the CID office again, where Jimmy and Inspector McManus were talking to a slight, grey-haired gentleman, who introduced himself to Mel as 'Martim Osvaldo Santos Luis da Silva – but please just call me Martim Silva!'

He asked what particular line of questioning he should follow, then Jimmy said, "Maybe it would be more straightforward if I simply ask him in English, and you can translate both ways – does this suit you? Let's go and see what he has to say. This way, Dr da Silva!"

The two inspectors and da Silva went to the interview room, collecting the shorthand writer on the way.

Alex was eager to learn what Melpomene had found out from Lady Hyacinth, and he was not disappointed when Mel related the conversation and finished, "We've got a very valuable source of information here, Alex – I reckon she's ready to spill the beans on a whole lot of people, starting with the two thugs who are in the habit of borrowing her Lagonda – she probably knows much more than she's said so far, and once she can be convinced that she's safe from retaliation from her husband and others she'll give us all sorts of good stuff!"

Alex agreed and added, "While you were in there, talking to Lady H, Jimmy told me that he had decided that whatever plot those two assailants who pushed Speedie to his death were being prepared for – they'd been brought back from the continent for some reason, after all – then all bets are off, now that Killane has been picked up. So he sent word to his people who are keeping vigil on the Saffron Walden house and ordered them to descend on the house in force and pick them up, together with whoever else seemed to be accomplices. We'll get word of the outcomes of this operation as soon as it has been concluded."

"What I'm waiting for," said Melpomene, "is whatever we can now find out about the other villains in the plot, such as Lord Ellsworth himself and his various bursars and assorted hangers-on. But they've probably been warned off since last night – I wouldn't be surprised if there hasn't been a general exodus!"

"Where would they go, Mel? Jimmy has put out a watch notice to the ports and aerodromes for Lord and Lady E, and also the Furlongs, who he would very much like to question, although we have no idea whether they are part of the plot or just beneficiaries of it. I also told him a few other names of people who we suspect are involved, such as the Bursar."

Chapter 47

After more than an hour, Dr da Silva, Jimmy Manley and Inspector McManus emerged, the shorthand writer saying, "I'll get this transcribed and typed up as soon as I can, Sir," as he disappeared with his notes.

The others came into the CID room and McManus said, "I've ordered coffee and biscuits all round – Dr da Silva needs some sustenance particularly, he's been working very hard. You must send us your bill, Dr – no doubt you have standard rates for interpreting?"

"Yes, Inspector, but I should say that this job was much more entertaining than what I usually have to deal with – nevertheless I shall still bill you!"

"So, Melpomene and Alex," said Jimmy, "you are probably all keyed up to hear what transpired. We'll send you a copy of the transcript, of course, but let me give you an outline now, with some of my interpretation, too. I should point out that we have only interrogated Senhor Branco so far, keeping Killane for later – what we have from this first interview will enable us to make our questioning of Killane much more pointed, and we shall not need an interpreter for him, anyway."

After helping himself to coffee and a vanilla cream biscuit, Jimmy went on.

"Our colleague, Sir Adrian Fitz-Hugh, of the fledgling international police service, will be particularly interested in Senhor Branco, because he told us that he and the late Coronel Oliveira were working for a Portuguese organized crime gang. It is similar to the Calabrian Ndrangheta or the Sicilian Mafia, but has not yet established itself as strongly as the Italian organizations, while steadily growing in its scope and power. Our two were sent to England with the aim of eliminating Killane, who had become an embarrassment to his employer, Lord Ellsworth – we are becoming convinced that he was the one who ordered the operation. As we now know, Killane was not inclined to be a victim and struck first! Branco has reacted very badly to this, and readily answered all our questions, hoping, I think, to be treated leniently as a result. He believes he has more to fear from the gang than from British justice, as organized criminals do not easily forgive failure."

"Did he actually name Ellsworth as his client?" asked Alex.

"No," replied Jimmy, "and he had nothing to say about Lord and Lady Furlong either. In my view, they represent prospective purchasers of the shares in the real estate of the university, rather than co-conspirators."

"I'm a little confused still, Jimmy," said Alex, "in his speech, Lord E said that the assets were being sold to a consortium in both England and Portugal – does this imply that the Portuguese gang has a financial interest in the transaction?"

"We are in process of finding out," said Jimmy, "as soon as I've been able to contact someone I know in the Fraud Squad at the Yard – whenever any major offering of shares is announced, whether in a private company like a university or a publicly-listed one, notifications have to be lodged with the Stock Exchange, and our experts routinely check them out. This way we can often save innocent and greedy investors from making major mistakes. Being located in the City, the fraud squad has a late start to its working day, so when I rang earlier there was nobody who could help me there. I'll try again, shortly."

"Before you do," said Melpomene, "I want to say thank you Jimmy for passing us a note about Irene Bradshaw being safe last night – what's the story with her?"

"A storm in a tea-cup, really, Mel, but it could have developed into something more serious. What happened was that yesterday afternoon she realised she needed an oil change and brake check for her car, so she took it to the garage where Lord Ellsworth has his car serviced, remembering that you two had picked up some useful information from a conversation between the mechanic there and Clive Sturgeon, Ellsworth's chauffeur. While she was booking her car in for the work, Lady Killane's Maroon Lagonda drove up, so Irene, who I think is fancying herself more and more as a detective, wandered over and engaged the driver in idle chat. I should point out that Lady K was not in the car at the time. The outcome was that he offered to drive her home while her car was being fixed, as she lives not far from the Killanes' place. He was pleasant enough, but she thought he looked at her rather hard a couple of times. The long and the short of it is that on the way, she started to panic that she was being abducted, told him she was getting car sick and asked him to set her down at some shops on the way. He was puzzled, but didn't argue, so she went into a chemist's shop till she was sure he had driven off! Then, would you believe, she walked to a tea-shop near by and consumed a hearty Devonshire cream tea before strolling home!"

"I shall have to tick her off next time I see her, about taking risks!" said Melpomene, "But perhaps the experience has made that point already! I'm sorry, Jimmy, I interrupted you to ask about Irene – what were you about to do?"

"Ring my oppo, Chief Inspector Saunders, at the Fraud Squad. Here goes – Millie, can you try that Fraud Squad number again? Ah, hello Miss, DI Manley of Mile End Road here, calling from Harpenden. Would CI Saunders be available? Ah, Frank, Jimmy Manley here. We're working on a case involving a possibly dodgy financial take-over of the real property of Harpenden University – would that sort of thing fall into your bailiwick? – Ah, very good, would you be able to cast your beady eyes over this business for us? I shall be back at Mile End Road after today. We're investigating one murder from last night already that seems to be relevant, and there was another a few weeks ago which made the headlines, when an unfortunate gentleman was pushed under an underground train, and so we want to lay hands on the major culprits before they disappear into the bushes or commit more. We're interested in Lord and Lady Ellsworth and possibly Lord and Lady Furlong, so this could get rather sensitive! We have the perpetrator from last night in the cells here at Harpenden nick, and we're about to subject him to the third degree, as they say in the Hollywood movies! I'll keep you informed, Frank. Look after yourself and we'll have a pint together some time!"

Mel said, "It sounds as though that side of things is well under control. As it's apparent that we can't be of any further help here, and you prefer us not to be present during the interrogation, we might slip away now. We'll call Irene and see whether she's back at work yet. With Killane safely under your protection here, we might be able to do some more rifling of his files – nothing illegal, of course, Jimmy!"

Irene was indeed back at her desk, and readily agreed to Mel's proposal.

"I've already had a more energetic poke around, and I found one document that might interest you very much! See you and Alex shortly – I'll have the kettle on and I bought some cakes at the teashop yesterday which won't be stale yet!"

Chapter 48

When they were sitting in Irene's office having tea and cakes, Alex asked, "So what was this fascinating document you found, Irene – and how did you come across it? – I thought the files had all been gone over pretty thoroughly between the three of us."

"For some reason, Alex, I recalled reading, years ago, an Edgar Allan Poe story called 'The Purloined Letter' – do you know it? In that story, an important letter was hidden by making it look like something inconsequential and putting it with other unimportant items. So I went and looked at Killane's desk and saw something – come and I'll show you!"

On the wall behind Killane's chair was a small notice-board, with several picture postcards from friends on holiday and reminder notes – such as 'Pick up wine on way home' and 'remember to ring Turnbull' – attached to it with drawing pins.

"And this was pinned up there, too!" said Irene, and showed Alex a scruffy dog-eared piece of folded paper. She opened it up and handed to him, so he could see it was a hand-written letter.

Alex read it out, "It's signed fairly illegibly, Mel – it could be 'Wilf' or 'Will', or even 'Wally'! and it reads as follows, *Dear Desmond, you'll be glad to hear that our two friends made it back from Lisbon, via The Hook, yesterday, and are safely resting in comfort at The Grange. We've made sure that they know nothing about the Furlongs – as far as they know, they were just working for you. Of course, stupid E revealed himself by taking them to Harwich, so his cover is blown – can't say I'd be worried if he gets picked up as a result, he'd be no great loss! Max and Sissie Furlong will be contacting you when they're here for E's dinner – be very careful what you tell them – of course, they already know all about Speedie! Don't mention this letter to H, I'm getting very nervous about her – she looks as though she could crack up any time!'* And that's where it ends. What wouldn't I give to know who sent it – Wilf or Wally or whatever his name is!"

"Can you think of anyone around the university with a name like that, Irene?" asked Melpomene, "I suppose 'Wally' is a diminutive for 'Walter', so are there any of those? Perhaps Gwyneth might be able to think of someone who could fit any of these – I'll give her a call."

"Oh Gwyneth, Melpomene here – by the way, thanks for finding us Dr da Silva, who did an excellent job of interpreting. Now we're trying to find someone who sent a letter to Killane, signing it 'Will' or 'Wilf' or possibly 'Wally' – it's almost illegible – anybody spring to mind?"

Gwyneth asked, "Does it have to be a man, because there is a Wilhelmina Parsons in the Bursar's office who calls herself 'Willy' and I'm wondering also whether the first letter was really a 'W', since some people write their 'M's like that when they're in a hurry. The Vice-Chancellor is Malcolm McArthur, so might it be 'Mal'? Have another look, and see whether that could be it – otherwise I'm at a loss for the moment, but if I think of anyone I'll let you know. I see you're both with Irene now."

They all had another look at the letter, squinting at various angles, but none of them could make the signature look anything like 'Mal'.

"Ah well, we'll just have to keep on the alert for someone who might fit," said Melpomene, "it could be a nickname, I suppose, which makes it even more obscure. I suppose we'd better get back home now – we had a late night for some reason, so I'll be ready for bed as soon as we get there. I'll ring and see whether a dinner can be arranged a bit early."

"Hello, is that Mrs M? You're back earlier than I expected – how are the mother and child? Oh, lovely! We'll be back in a couple of hours and we'd like to eat almost as soon as we arrive – can that be managed? We were up till all hours last night!"

Alex said, "Before we set off, I'll give the office a call, to let them know we're on our way back to London, and see if there have been any messages for us."

Winnie and Marjorie had nothing much to report, except that Adrian Fitz-Hugh had called, saying he had some more information about the Portuguese people, but that it would keep. The secretaries said they could force themselves to wait until the next day for the news from Harpenden, but would expect a full account then, with actions and appropriate voices.

All went as planned, and they again slept very well, so the next morning after breakfast both Melpomene and Alex were bright-eyed and bushy-tailed and arrived at the office ready to go.

Mel told the girls that, of course they would hear the full story with dramatic embellishments, but she wanted to ring Jimmy Manley first, and Alex said that while she was doing that he would see whether Adrian Fitz-Hugh was available and get his update on the Portuguese men.

"Good morning, Jimmy, I'm eager to hear how your interrogation of Killane went – did he spill anything sensational?"

"Quite a lot, Mel! I suppose you are in your office now – why don't I drop round and tell you what Jock McManus and I managed to extract between us, and also give you the latest news from Saffron Walden – see you soon."

Alex was still on the telephone to Fitz-Hugh, so Mel said, "Tea and jam tarts, ladies – I do hope there are jam tarts! – and then all the tales can be told! Jimmy Manley will be here soon."

Alex hung up and announced that Adrian had said that he was happy that he would be able to close his file on Coronel Gustavo Oliveira, but that he still hadn't been able to get much on Senhor Castelo Branco. Alex told him that Branco had been interrogated at Harpenden police station, and that they were expecting a transcript to be sent, and he would see that Adrian got a copy.

"Any more calls or letters this morning?" he asked, and Marjorie said, "Nothing exciting, just bills, bills and a nice card about baby Christabel from Mrs Mountain's daughter. And Archie Staples just rang while Alex was on the telephone, and said that since he wanted to speak to Alex particularly, he would call again in a little while."

As promised, Melpomene entertained the secretaries with a graphic reenactment of the events at the Blue Boar, 'doing the police in different voices' and with sound effects of pistol shots and everything.

The girls applauded enthusiastically, and Winnie said, "This makes me even more glad that I switched careers – neither the dentist's or the estate agent's office were anything like as exciting as it has been here in just a few short weeks!"

Chapter 49

Jimmy Manley arrived and immediately asked, "Can I use your telephone, please? I had a call from Frank Saunders' office at the Fraud Squad as I was leaving, so I said I would get back to him as soon as I arrived here. Here we go – can I speak to Detective Inspector Saunders please, DI Manley from Mile End Road here. Oh hello, Frank, sorry about that, I was literally on my way out of the door when your assistant rang and I'm now at the offices of Crabbe and Crabbe, the private detectives who are the driving force in the Harpenden University case. Did you manage to discover anything? Oh, wonderful! I'll let you talk to Alex Crabbe directly, because he has all the details at his fingertips."

Jimmy turned to the others and said, "Where's my cup of tea, then? Oh good, jam tarts, too, excellent! I expect, Mel, that you will be interested in what we got out of our interviews with Senhor Castelo Branco and Sir Desmond Killane, am I right? I've brought copies of the verbatim transcripts for you, all nicely typed up, but I'll tell you the important bits now. Alex can catch up when he comes off the telephone with Frank Saunders."

"Off you go, then, Jimmy – Marjorie and Winnie will be interested, too!"

"I was a little disappointed with Branco actually – as you will recall, Mel, he was considerably shaken up when we took him to the station, and would probably have blabbed freely then, but by the time our interpreter arrived the next morning he had composed himself – so we probably got a highly edited and considered version. Nevertheless, there was still some useful information in it. He confirmed what we had suspected, that he and the Coronel had been brought here to eliminate Desmond Killane – but he had turned out not to be the sitting duck they had expected!"

"Did he say who had been behind this plan?" asked Mel.

"No – this was where he had decided to be cagy – even when I suggested some names, he didn't rise to the bait. I mentioned Ellsworth, Vice-Chancellor McArthur and even Henry Hanson, the Bursar, but he didn't twitch an eyebrow at any of these, either when I said them or when the interpreter repeated them. I'm beginning to think there might be a master villain lurking in the shadows and playing all these people like puppets! I even asked Branco straight out whose orders they were following – he wouldn't say but I think he was worried by the question. Perhaps it was a higher-up in their organization who instructed them, while the name of the ultimate client was never disclosed. There is more detail in the transcript, but those are the main points as I see them, Mel."

"Thanks, Jimmy – here's Alex off his telephone call. What did the fraud people tell you, Alex?"

"A lot of it went over my head – we've really opened a can of worms here! Frank Saunders says that the long and short of it is that Harpenden University is headed for bankruptcy! It runs a number of accounts at different banks, which is an indication that not all is above-board, and a trustee group, which appears to be constituted mainly of members of the Senate, has requested investigation of its affairs by appealing to the Chancery Court. I'm afraid that I managed to avoid these areas during my law studies, so I don't fully understand all this. Be that as it may, it is clear that something will soon have to change before the proposed lease of the buildings and campus to a consortium can go ahead. And, Frank suggested, if it is discovered that Lord Ellsworth or his associates have deliberately infringed the regulations they will be held accountable and charged under the appropriate laws. This is all on top of any embezzlement charges that will be brought against Killane or anyone else who have had their hands in the till!"

"So does this mean that we can leave the courts to deal with all the financial matters and arrest Lord Ellsworth and his collaborators?" asked Melpomene.

Jimmy answered her, "Right, but you and my colleagues between us still have a number of other matters to follow up – not the least of them at least two murders! No doubt you will want to know about what went off at The Grange, Saffron Walden – as I said yesterday, I called for a full-scale raid on that house, all officers to be armed, with instructions to pick up the two who disposed of Cyril Speedie and anyone else who could have been involved. In the event, they bagged red-nose and his mate who we've been calling the bank manager, and four others, two of whom were so foolish as to draw pistols on our men. But they were swiftly disarmed, cuffed and stowed away in our vans. The other people in the house were mainly domestic servants, so we just took their names and home addresses and sent them away. The house has been sealed, and our forensic specialists will run their fine-toothed combs over it over the next day or two."

Melpomene asked, "What about the other heavies – the red-head and his friend who we spotted in Lady Hyacinth's Lagonda – they brought her car back so they are now somewhere around the Harpenden area I should think."

"Ah yes – well, Lady H is all cooperation now and readily gave us their names and addresses, so they've probably already been picked up by Jock McManus and his men. They'll likely be charged as accessories, before and after the fact, to the murder of Cyril Speedie."

"And Senhor Branco?" asked Alex, "he certainly assaulted Desmond Killane will he be charged with that? He'll plead self-defence I suppose."

"Not to mention conspiracy to commit murder, going armed in company with the intent to commit a felony, and anything else we can nail him for – remember, he and the Coronel are part of an international criminal organization!" said Jimmy, with some satisfaction. "And we mustn't forget that Killane shot and killed Coronel Oliveira, on top of being an embezzler!"

Alex chuckled, "There's going to be weeks and weeks of court cases now – Mel and I had better get special outfits for our appearances as witnesses! By the way, didn't Archie Staples say he was going to call us this morning?"

Marjorie said, "He could have tried when our telephones were tied up – should I try his number?"

He was found, and Marjorie passed the telephone to Alex, to hear Archie say "Yes, I tried both your numbers in turn, so I'm glad you've rung me. What I wanted to tell you about was a recent exploit of Daniel Flint, KC. As you know, his sister is married to Sir Desmond Killane, but their marriage is going through a sticky patch, apparently. So Flint got on to one of his solicitor contacts and suggested that Hyacinth might be in need of a good divorce lawyer soon and suggested that the solicitor get in touch and offer his services. Now this is unprofessional conduct, so the legal authorities were informed, and Flint has been summoned to attend a hearing to defend himself!"

Chapter 50

Four days later, on the afternoon before Christmas Eve, a small procession of cars turned in at the gates of the Woodhampton Castle Hotel. Melpomene and Alex were accompanied by Pat Georgiadis and Winnie Morris – Marjorie Wentworth had chosen to spend Christmas with her Mum and Dad. Following was Irene Bradshaw, with Olive and Gwyneth Fletcher and Angela Dayton, and bringing up the rear was the big Rover of Betty and Archie Staples, who had given a lift to DC Cecil Thomson and his wife Christine.

At the porte-cochère, the luggage was taken by hotel porters and they were all ushered into the entrance hall. Then Lady Cynthia, Melpomene's Mama, rushed up and embraced everyone she knew and was introduced to those she didn't.

"Aren't Jimmy Manley and his family coming this time, Mel dear?" she asked, and was told, "No, Mama, apparently Jimmy's Mum has put her foot down and said that she doesn't see enough of them and she's missing her grandchildren! But you haven't met Jimmy's colleague Cecil and his wife, Christine, so we'll have a police presence all the same!"

"And, of course, the local force will be represented, dear – we couldn't leave out David Wilkinson and his wife – and we'll also see the Buckmasters here on Christmas day. Now, please point out to the staff which cases belong to which people. Apart from the married couples, who were easy to sort out, we've put Olive and Gwyneth together in the room at the front with the piano, because they will need somewhere to rehearse, of course – they needn't think they are going to get away without singing to us all, now that Mel and Alex have told us about their talent! And Pat is in with Angela and Irene with Winifred – is that acceptable, ladies? We can do a bit of shuffling if anyone finds they hate their room-mate! Dinner tonight is very informal – come down any time after seven, no need to dress."

Lady Cynthia happily waved all her guests away but turned to Melpomene and Alex, saying, "Before you two disappear to get ready for dinner, we have some catching-up to do! The last I heard from you was the day after the astonishing scenes at the Blue Boar, when you were setting off back to London from Harpenden – has anything happened since then that would interest me? – I think so! Come and get comfortable in my sitting-room and we can have a glass of something while you tell me all!"

So Mel and Alex related the subsequent events and told Lady Cynthia what various people had reported to them.

"So, does it look as though the university will survive in some form – it would be a tragedy if so many students had their lives disrupted, would it not?"

Alex agreed, but assured her that it was not that easy to abolish such an institution, and that companies often rise from the ashes, phoenix-like, after going bankrupt or being taken over.

Back in their familiar suite, Melpomene had a bath and Alex took his turn while Mel was wondering what to wear for dinner.

As they were about to make their way to the dining-room, the telephone rang, and the hotel operator said to Melpomene, "I have a Colonel Stavely-Roper on the line, who would like to speak to Mr Alex or you, Madam, is that all right?"

"Certainly!" Mel passed the telephone to Alex, who said, "Nice to hear from you, Randolph – the compliments of the season to you. What can we do for you?"

"I found where you were from your secretary, Miss Wentworth. I called to let you know about the latest developments here at Harpenden. As you may know, a group of trustees, mainly members of Senate, convened by yours truly, enquired whether the court of Chancery could intervene – as a result, the officers of the court started a thorough process of investigation. The upshot is that the affairs of the university have been placed in the hands of a large accountancy firm in the City acting as official receiver, and an application for bankruptcy is in train!"

"So what has happened to Lord Ellsworth and his disreputable tribe?"

"All sacked – and some, including Ellsworth, in gaol, charged with serious offences! I have had the honour of being appointed as the interim Vice-Chancellor – with no deputy! – and the new Bursar is none other than your friend Irene Bradshaw! She was chosen because she kept tabs on all that was going on while she was Killane's personal assistant – she is, as you might know, a qualified accountant. The trustees also decided to meet all the bills for time and expenses submitted to them by Crabbe and Crabbe!"

"My word, Randolph – you've got everything under control already – most impressive! Thank you very much for all that!"

Mel was equally impressed when Alex passed this all on, "I can now go on with the Christmas festivities with my mind at rest!" she said, "Let's make some announcements at dinner this evening, and then we can all enjoy ourselves! But I'm going to go and congratulate Irene right now – coming?"

Irene was very happy when Mel hugged her and wished her well in her new life, "I have nearly been bursting to tell everyone in sight – but forced myself to wait until it was official, so to speak! Of course I'm a little apprehensive – but I console myself by the knowledge that the last incumbent made a real hoo-ha of the job, beside exploiting the funds whenever he could do so!"

The dinner became a very jovial affair after all this new information was absorbed by everyone. As Lady Cynthia said, "We can all celebrate Christmas with nothing to distract us now, thanks to the efforts of many of our guests who arrived today, not to mention those others who weren't able to join us here, for one reason and another, so let's all raise our glasses and make a traditional toast – 'to absent friends'!"

During a quiet moment, Alex turned to Mel and said, "I've got mixed feelings about having no case at the moment – part of me looks forward to a rest, and the other yearns for a new job!"

"I know what you mean!" said Melpomene, "But I should tell you that I received a letter in the hotel mail this morning from an old friend from our days at LSE. I haven't seen her in ages, but we used go around together a lot. I didn't even know that she was married, but she says that she is getting worried – her in-laws are becoming very hostile to her, and her husband, who is a stock-broker, is looking very out of sorts – he has stopped playing sports, and he sits around saying nothing. When she tries to ask him what's the matter, he snaps at her! I think I shall telephone her in a day or two, once the Christmas festivities are out of the way, because it seems, reading between the lines, that she would like me to look into this! So maybe this could turn out to be Crabbe and Crabbe's next case!"

FIN

KEEP VIGILANT FOR THE NEXT CASE!

Crabbe and Crabbe's next case will be coming out soon!

Will there be murders? Who knows.

Will there be skulduggery? Undoubtedly.

Will Melpomene and Alex solve the case?

Of course – how could anyone doubt this!

Look out for:

"Exchange is no Robbery"
A Case for Crabbe and Crabbe.

By Geoffrey Foster

Coming later this year.